LOVE AND ILLNESS FIND PEMBERLEY: BOOK 1 OF 4

Jane Austen's Pride and Prejudice Clean and wholesome Continuation

This book is a work of fiction. Names, characters, places and incidents are either the product of the author's imagination or are used fictionally. Any resemblance to actual persons, living or dead, or to actual events or locales is entirely coincidental.

First printing, 2020

Publisher

His Everlasting Love Media

info@hiseverlastinglove.com

www.HisEverlastingLove.com

❀ Created with Vellum

ADDITIONAL INFORMATION

Please check the back of the book for the following:

- Information on how to receive a free book
- Our "About the Author" page
- A list of other books by His Everlasting Love Media

CHAPTER 1

"'My dearest Elizabeth,'" Elizabeth began, reading the letter in her hand and catching the lifted eyebrow of her husband. "'I am so very glad to know that you have returned from your honeymoon and have settled well in Pemberley. It sounds like you have had a marvelous time, and I shall be sure to inform our friends here in Meryton of all you have done and achieved.'"

Mr. Darcy picked up his toast and took a bite, chewing it carefully but making no comment. Elizabeth smiled at him, knowing full well what he was thinking. In telling such news, it would not be for Elizabeth's benefit, nor for that of their dear friends in Meryton, but rather for Mrs. Bennet's benefit alone. She would revel in the joy and importance that came with her daughter being married to so eligible a gentleman as Mr. Darcy and would make quite certain that everyone near to her knew of it.

"'However, since your marriage, I must tell you that Kitty has become greatly downhearted,'" she continued, reading her mother's letter carefully. "'Your father, as you know, is much too severe with her and refuses to allow her to visit any friends without my presence. I, of course, am much too tired to make my way to Meryton every day, and Mary steadfastly refuses to go with her sister, finding it to be a poor use of her time.'"

"On this, I think I agree with your sister Mary," Mr. Darcy murmured, making Elizabeth laugh. "There would be much better things for Catherine to do instead of running around Meryton in search of her friends."

"That is hardly fair," Elizabeth replied. "We have some excellent acquaintances in Meryton, although I *will* admit that there are some who are very foolish indeed." She sighed and looked down at her letter. "Father has not relented in any way, it seems. Although I cannot pretend that I believe it to be a bad decision on his part."

Darcy nodded, his expression a little grim as he recalled the events of the previous few months. "Indeed," he said, pointing to the letter with the toast in his hand. "What else does your mother write?"

With a smile still playing about her lips, Elizabeth picked up the letter once more and tried to find her place. "Ah, yes. She states, 'Your father has, however, agreed to allow Kitty to come and stay with you for an extended time, should you be willing to have her. I would, of course, like to send Mary also, but that may be too much for you to bear. It would mean a great deal to both of your sisters, I am sure, and certainly would bring a great deal of pleasure to me also—since your father is being most severe. I am, of course, your ever-loving mother and...'" Elizabeth trailed off, her brows knitting together. "There are a few sentiments and other such things, but she does not say anything further of importance."

Mr. Darcy let out a long breath and set down his teacup, clearly now replete. "I will be honest with you, my dear, since I know that you will not expect anything less from me." Clearing his throat, he smiled rather ruefully. "I would prefer not to have your two sisters here with us, but I shall not refuse to have them."

"That would be uncharitable," Elizabeth replied with a twinkle in her eye. "I confess that I have the very same feelings as you on the subject." Taking in a breath, she considered things carefully. "It has been something of a freedom to be without my sisters *and* my mother," she confessed. "Although I miss Jane, of course."

"Of course," Mr. Darcy replied with a warm smile.

"But to state that my—as yet—unmarried sisters are not welcome here would be, as I have said, uncharitable," she finished, with a small shake of her head. "We must, of course, invite them to stay for a short time."

Mr. Darcy tilted his head and regarded Elizabeth carefully. "A *short* time, yes."

Elizabeth laughed wryly and rose from the table to go in search of the writing desk. "I do not think either one of us could abide their company for too long," she said, pressing his shoulder gently as she passed. "It will not be for a long duration; I assure you."

Reaching to catch her hand before she lifted it, Mr. Darcy brought it to his mouth and kissed her palm gently. "I trust your judgement entirely, my dear."

This made Elizabeth flush with pleasure, and she smiled at him, letting her gaze linger on him as he held her eyes with his. He was so very handsome, she considered, but the way he had shown such kindness and generosity to both herself and her family made him all the more wonderful in her eyes.

"You do not regret marrying me?" Mr. Darcy asked.

Reaching down, she touched his cheek gently. "Of course I do not regret it," Elizabeth told him, speaking the truth with her every word. "I could *never* regret it. You know that my feelings have changed in every way and that my heart is now yours."

The way his eyes lit at such a statement made her heart sing. "As mine is yours," he told her, finally releasing her hand. "Go. Write to your mother. And inform me the moment you receive her reply."

"I shall do that," Elizabeth replied, bending down to kiss him lightly on the mouth before making her way from the room, a lightness in her spirits that added a joy to her every step.

~

"I can see the carriage," Elizabeth said, her voice filled with both excitement and trepidation.

Elizabeth leaned into Mr. Darcy, as he came to stand by her side, knowing that they would both need a good deal of strength for the days that were to follow. This was not precisely what Elizabeth had anticipated when she had returned to Pemberley as the wife of Mr. Darcy. She had foreseen months of just herself and Darcy, settling down as husband and wife, becoming used to living in Pemberley, exploring the grounds, and making this place her home. Instead, she was now to share it with her two sisters, who—apparently—were finding it difficult being at home under their father's new strict rules.

Mary would not be particularly difficult, given that Darcy had an extensive library, which would provide a great deal of distraction for her. Kitty, on the other hand, would demand attention and outings and all manner of things to keep her entertained—not that Elizabeth had any intention of doing such a thing, however.

Kitty would have to learn that Elizabeth was not about to do whatever was required just to keep her content. Pemberley was a place for quietness, for reflection, for walking and enjoying the outdoors. Kitty would not appreciate it, perhaps, but—in time—Elizabeth hoped that she would come to do so.

"Here they come," Mr. Darcy murmured, as Elizabeth raised her head from his shoulder. "Goodness, what droll expressions they wear!"

"I am sure they are merely overwhelmed with the house," Elizabeth replied with a smile, as the carriage door was held open for the ladies by a footman.

Leaving Mr. Darcy at the very top step, Elizabeth hurried down the stone steps to meet her sisters, her hands outstretched. "Mary!" she said, welcoming her with a quick embrace. "And Kitty. Welcome to Pemberley. I do hope that your journey was not particularly arduous?"

Mary blinked in the sunshine, as she regarded the house and said, "We have made it here without difficulty, thanks to the grace of God."

"I have found it *most* uncomfortable," Kitty protested, screwing up her face as she looked up at Mr. Darcy. "At least we are here now, I suppose." She smiled at Elizabeth, who held her gaze for a moment, trying to assess her sister. "Might we go inside now?"

"Yes, of course," Elizabeth replied, trying not to be piqued by her sister's rude manner. "Do greet Darcy, Kitty. Recall now that you are to be as polite and as considerate towards him as you are with anyone."

Kitty laughed and fluttered a hand, evidently not requiring any particular advice. She said nothing but hurried up the steps, greeting Mr. Darcy quickly before turning to go into the house. Mr. Darcy, who had not yet greeted Mary, threw a quick glance after Kitty before welcoming Mary.

"Kitty!" Elizabeth, already frustrated, hurried after her sister, wishing she had not been so rude.

To walk into another person's house without being led in by the host or hostess was more than a little improper, but when had Elizabeth ever expected Kitty to act with decorum? Leaving Mary to walk with Mr. Darcy, Elizabeth hurried into the entrance hall, seeing Kitty staring, wide eyed, at all that lay before her.

"Kitty," Elizabeth said, irritation flooding her voice. "You cannot simply walk in ahead of Darcy. Surely you must know how improper that is." Seeing how Kitty was still staring at the house and not giving her the least bit of attention, Elizabeth pushed down her own frustration and then continued, "You must be tired after your journey. Shall I show you to your room? You can rest and change there—if you wish?"

Kitty laughed and twirled around. "No, I should not like to rest!" she exclaimed, throwing a teasing look towards Elizabeth. "I have been in the carriage for a very long time, and I cannot imagine resting now! I must walk and explore and enjoy all that is here!"

"Whereas I should certainly like to rest," Mary interrupted, coming in behind Elizabeth. "I find myself quite weary."

Elizabeth, a little relieved that she would have only one sister to deal with, turned to smile at Mary. "I shall show you to your room, Mary. Mr. Darcy also has an extensive library, which I am sure you shall find great delight in."

"And you are welcome to explore it whenever you wish," Darcy added, making both Mary and Kitty look at him in astonishment, clearly taken aback by his welcoming tone. "I insist upon it, Miss Bennet."

A small smile tugged at Mary's mouth. "I think you are permitted to call me 'Mary' now, Mr. Darcy," she replied, making Mr. Darcy clear his throat and place his hands behind his back, clearly a little embarrassed. "And I thank you for your very generous offer. I confess that this was something I hoped for in coming to visit you. Your library will be much greater than my father's, I think."

"Oh, Mary," Kitty said with a laugh, her voice echoing around the entrance hall. "Of course it will be. You are so very ridiculous sometimes."

Elizabeth closed her eyes and drew in a long breath before she turned to speak to her sister. "Kitty, come with me. I shall show you around Pemberley and then, perhaps after that, you will feel more inclined to rest." She shot a smile towards Darcy, who looked a little relieved. "We shall take Mary to her room, and thereafter, I will allow you to explore the house." Looking back at Mary, she smiled gently. "And would you like some refreshments before you rest, Mary? Some tea and cake, perhaps?"

Mary nodded, looking rather pleased with this suggestion. "Thank you, Elizabeth."

"Come then," Elizabeth replied, making her way to the staircase that would lead to the next floor and, a little further along, the bedchambers. "We will see you for dinner, Darcy."

Darcy smiled at her, his eyes twinkling, garnering another surprised look from both Kitty and Mary, who both still thought him very severe indeed.

"Until then," he said, inclining his head to all the ladies before stepping away, clearly relieved that he would not have to be with Kitty for the duration of the afternoon.

With a smile on her face, Elizabeth led both Mary and Kitty up the staircase, finding herself both glad and a little frustrated that they were both, once more, within her company. She knew that, depending on Kitty's behavior, this next month might be very difficult indeed.

CHAPTER 2

The first sennight with Elizabeth's two sisters was something of a blur. Mary spent most of her time in the library, and in the evening, she regaled them with all that she had been reading. It was often a further study on a certain passage of the Bible, which—whilst interesting at times—often came across as rather moralizing.

Kitty, of course, was very often bored by such conversation and made her feelings on the matter well known, meaning that sharp words could often be exchanged between the two sisters. This, in turn, wearied both Elizabeth and Mr. Darcy, who did their best to keep silent, only speaking when things became a little too tense.

During the day, Kitty complained about her lack of entertainment, questioned whether any soldiers would come anywhere near Pemberley, and cried about Lydia's evident unwillingness to reply to the many letters that Kitty sent. This, however, Elizabeth could well understand, for she felt the separation from Jane to be a very difficult one indeed—even though they were both happily married and very content.

However, knowing that there were at least four weeks remaining for her sisters' visit, Elizabeth decided that something must be done about Kitty's ridiculous behavior. Yes, Kitty's character had begun to improve as a result of her separation from Lydia, but *clearly* even being in Lydia's company again during both Jane and Elizabeth's wedding had sent Kitty back to her usual self. It would take time and effort—and effort was something Elizabeth was willing to give.

"What will you do with her?" Mr. Darcy asked, his fingers brushing over her arm as they sat together on the couch.

They were listening to Mary play the pianoforte whilst Kitty stared dully into the fire burning in the fireplace. Thankfully, Mary's playing had been much improved of late, perhaps due to the fact that her mother no longer doted upon Jane and Lydia. She did not sing, however, and that was something for which Elizabeth was rather grateful.

Mr. Darcy touched her fingers with his own. "Do you intend to speak with her?" he asked.

Elizabeth sighed heavily and looked up at him. "There is nothing else I can do," she said, with a small shrug of her shoulder. "It is not as though she has ever listened to me before, but perhaps, without Lydia, there is a chance that she might do so now."

Darcy smiled at her, his eyes glowing with what Elizabeth knew to be love. "If anyone can convince her to change her ways, to examine herself and to perhaps reconsider her behavior, it will be you, my dear," he said.

A small smile quirked the corner of Elizabeth's lips. "Do you not fear I shall be too blunt, too outspoken, and too harsh with my words? To the point that I might accidentally drive her far from me?" she asked tenderly, recalling her own behavior towards him some time ago.

"No," he answered, taking her hand in his and squeezing it gently. "I think you will do very well indeed, my love. Just as you have done with me."

~

The following morning, when Mary had taken leave of the breakfast table in order to ensconce herself in the library once more, Elizabeth chose to speak directly to her sister Kitty.

"Kitty," Elizabeth began, seeing how her sister toyed with her food rather than lifting any to her mouth. "When I first received the letter from Mama, I confess I was not at all inclined to have you present with us. However, I chose to do so simply because I thought it would be an opportunity for both you and Mary to have time away from home and to enjoy all that Pemberley has to offer." She smiled tightly at her sister, keeping her voice steady and calm. "However, this last sennight, you have not shown any interest in the things that I have suggested."

"That is because I am *tired* of walking," Kitty complained with a toss of her head. "I am sure Pemberley is very lovely indeed, but one can only walk so far before becoming very bored."

Taking a moment to keep herself calm, Elizabeth let out a slow breath before she continued and said, "We can take the carriage to Lambton—if you wish. Or explore a little further if you would like. However, Kitty,"—she took a deep breath, looking directly at her sister and keeping her voice grave—"this continual complaining, the frustration that practically exudes from you with every suggestion that I make, *must* come to an end. In fact, you must work on changing your character, Kitty. Nothing will become of you if you do not do so."

Kitty rolled her eyes and leaned her head back, letting out a groan as she did so. "I do not want you to speak to me as Father does, Lizzie," she said and let out a sigh, looking back at her with irritation. "I thought I would find a little more excitement here, a little more freedom, but there is nothing to do other than to walk or to read! Mary might be content here, but I am not!"

"Then what would you wish to do?" Elizabeth asked, trying to battle her own frustration and anger rather than allowing it to show on her face and in her voice. Kitty would never listen to her if she became irate. "If you would prefer to return to Longbourn, then I would be happy to arrange such a thing."

"No!" Kitty exclaimed. Kitty's face suddenly became animated. Her color faded quickly, and she pressed both hands tightly together, the tips of her fingers pressing to her mouth.

The exclamation surprised Elizabeth and made her begin to wonder at the sudden change in her sister's expression. Was there more to Kitty's complaining than she had first thought?

"Kitty?" Elizabeth asked, as she rose to her feet and came over to the other side of the dining table, sitting down by her sister so that they might be a little closer and so that she could look into her sister's face a little more fully. "Whatever is wrong?"

Swallowing hard, Kitty kept her face away from Elizabeth's, giving a small shake of her head. "There is nothing wrong," she said quickly, dropping her gaze to her plate. "I just cannot imagine returning to Longbourn as yet, not when Father is so very strict."

Elizabeth did not believe her, especially seeing the tenseness in Kitty's shoulders and the way her gaze slid away from Elizabeth all the more.

"Kitty," she said gently. "I know very well that something is troubling you. It cannot only be that Father is rather changed of late. Is it that you find the household rather altered now that we are all gone away, save for Mary?"

Kitty finally glanced up, her eyes meeting Elizabeth's. "It is markedly changed," she said with a slight lift of one shoulder. "It is rather dull, in fact, given that Mary never wishes to step out of the house and Mama does nothing but sing the praises of both you and Jane." Her lips pursed for a moment, a small line forming between her brows. "It is as though Lydia has forgotten me entirely, and I am left all alone."

"Loneliness can be difficult," Elizabeth answered, honesty pouring forth. "And the thought of returning to that is troubling to you?"

Kitty gave her a sidelong glance. "It is," she slowly answered—after a long pause. "That is all."

Elizabeth frowned, but Kitty looked away quickly, making Elizabeth believe that, once again, her sister was not telling her the truth. But to press Kitty further would not, Elizabeth believed, bring any further benefit to either of them, and thus, Elizabeth lapsed into silence for a few minutes. Kitty also said nothing. Instead, she took to regarding her plate as though it was very interesting indeed.

"I shall not send you back, Kitty," Elizabeth told her, breaking the quiet. "In fact, should you wish to stay a little longer, then I am sure that can be arranged." She caught the way Kitty's eyes flared wide, as she glanced up at her quickly. There was an expression that crossed her sister's face, which was then hurriedly wiped away, as if it never existed. "But whenever you feel as though you are able to tell me the truth, Kitty, I will be glad to listen. I know that you have not told me all that is troubling you."

Her sister said nothing but kept her eyes downcast.

"However," Elizabeth continued, her voice taking on a little more severity. "I shall not permit you to continue to behave in this ridiculous manner, Kitty. You are here as our *guest*—and to continually complain about what you are dissatisfied about is rude at best."

"I understand," Kitty replied rather meekly. "I am sorry I have been ungrateful."

Surprised at Kitty's willingness to apologize, it took Elizabeth a moment to reply.

"Thank you, Kitty," she said gently. "Now, what would you like to do today?" She watched Kitty closely but was all the more astonished when Kitty shook her head and rose quietly from the table, seeming very sorrowful indeed.

"I should prefer to retire to my room for a time," she told Elizabeth, who also rose to her feet. "If you would not mind?"

"No, of course not," Elizabeth replied, reaching for Kitty's hand. "But are you sure you—?"

Kitty did not take Elizabeth's hand but stepped away, her hands clasped and her head rather low. "Thank you, Lizzie."

Elizabeth frowned hard as she watched Kitty leave. Kitty's demeanor had suddenly changed, and Elizabeth was not at all certain as to the reason why. Regardless, it concerned her that her sister had altered herself so greatly and so quickly.

"Lizzie?" said a familiar male voice.

She looked around to see none other than Mr. Darcy enter the room, coming towards her quickly.

“How was your conversation with Kitty?” he asked, looking at Elizabeth. “Do you think you have made any progress with her?”

“I-I am not sure,” Elizabeth replied truthfully, linking arms with him and walking through the dining room and into the long hallway. “I mentioned that she could return home...and that seemed to greatly trouble her.”

Mr. Darcy smiled and said, “Surely that is to be expected, especially given that your father has changed his expectations as to your sister’s behavior and what she is now permitted or not permitted to do?”

“In one way, yes,” Elizabeth answered, “but there is more to her difficulties than she is allowing me to be aware of at present.” She looked at her husband and gave him a rueful smile. “She did not want to tell me anything of it as yet, but I hope that in time she will.”

“It is good of you to give her time,” Darcy told her gently. “I am sure that she will tell you everything very soon.”

Elizabeth sighed gently and said, “We have never been particularly close as sisters, but I hope that she will still be willing to talk to me.”

“And with that,” Darcy replied, a trifle uneasily, “I did wonder if you would be willing to speak to Mary.”

Stopping suddenly, Elizabeth looked at her husband in surprise. “Mary?” she repeated, feeling herself a little weary. “Why ever would you wish me to do so? Is she not fully content either?”

"Yes, by all appearances, certainly," Darcy replied carefully, reaching out to take Elizabeth's hand in his. "I am not certain if you are aware of this, my dear, but Mary has been receiving a letter almost every day since she arrived."

Elizabeth lifted her eyebrows in astonishment. "Indeed? I did not think Mama would be that diligent."

A twinkle appeared in Mr. Darcy's eye. "Are you quite certain the letters can only come from your mother?" he asked, teasing her. "Surely if your mother had written to Mary, she would also have included notes to both you and to Kitty? Why would she *only* write to Mary?"

Realizing what Mr. Darcy was suggesting, Elizabeth stared at him in complete amazement. Such was the depths of her surprise that it took some time for her to reply. In the meantime, while Elizabeth collected her thoughts, Mr. Darcy began to chuckle.

"It cannot be that astonishing, my dear!" Mr. Darcy replied, reaching out and touching her cheek. "Mary might be a quiet, bookish sort, but there are gentlemen, I am sure, who would find such a thing to be...desirable in a wife."

"No indeed, I cannot believe it," Elizabeth replied with a shake of her head. "Mary would not entertain such a thing, I am sure."

Mr. Darcy laughed aloud, making Elizabeth smile self-consciously. "What can you mean, my dear lady?" he asked with a smile. "Do you think that Mary seeks to be a spinster? That she would not welcome the opportunity to be a wife and a mother should the opportunity be given her?"

It was not something Elizabeth had ever truly considered, for Mary had always shunned the chance to meet the militia, to dance, or to involve herself in any way with any suitable gentlemen. "Where would she have met such a gentleman?" she asked, turning to loop her hand through Darcy's again. "I cannot imagine that she—"

"There have been weddings recently," Mr. Darcy reminded her, giving her a gentle smile. "And there were gentlemen aplenty there."

Elizabeth blinked rapidly, trying to even *consider* the idea that Mary might now be being sought out by a suitable gentleman.

"I think it would be wise to perhaps *ask* who such letters are from," Mr. Darcy continued, reaching into his pocket and handing her a letter. "This one arrived only a half hour ago."

Elizabeth took it at once, looking at it with a sharp eye, but she could not make out the hand or the seal.

"Very well," she answered, as Darcy smiled at her, clearly a little relieved. "You are right to suggest that we become, at the very least, aware of such things. I do hope she has not—" The idea that came into her thoughts made her laugh at her foolishness.

"What is it?" Mr. Darcy asked, looking at her with interest. "Why do you laugh?"

Again, she shook her head. "It was only a thought that she has sought to write to this gentleman now—only because she is away from Longbourn, where Father cannot notice the correspondence between them," she said with a wry smile. "Foolishness, of course."

To her surprise, Mr. Darcy did not immediately agree that it was, indeed, a foolish thought. "But what if that is precisely what she has done?" he asked, as they came to a stop just outside the library. His eyes gleamed, as he smiled at her again, bending his head to kiss her forehead lightly. "I am eagerly expecting to hear more on all that you have been speaking of, my dear Lizzie. This visit of your sisters might turn out to be a little more interesting than I first thought!"

Elizabeth shook her head and laughed, before turning towards the library and rapping lightly, then stepping inside. Initially, she could not see Mary, but eventually, she spotted her in the corner of the library next to the window where the light was the best.

"Ah, Mary," Elizabeth said warmly, coming towards her sister. "I am sorry to disturb you, but a letter has arrived for you."

She looked at Mary steadily, as she held out the letter, but Mary reached for it without a word.

Placing it on the small table beside her, she gave Elizabeth a quick smile before turning her gaze back to her book.

"Mary," Elizabeth continued, now beginning to feel a little awkward. "The letters, I believe, have been coming for you very regularly."

Again, Mary looked up, nodded, but did not speak a word. With a quick smile, she looked back down at her book, leaving Elizabeth standing alone and quiet. Mary had never been a great conversationalist, but even this was rather unusual for her.

"Mary," Elizabeth said again, coming to sit down opposite her sister. "Mary, might I enquire as to whom these letters have come from?"

Looking up, Mary appeared a little surprised at this particular question. "I do not think it is appropriate for you to ask such a thing, Lizzie. Are you not being a little...impolite?"

Biting her lip and trying to choose her words carefully, Elizabeth took a moment before she replied. "The reason I ask,

Mary, is not to be impolite but rather because I am a little…concerned."

"Concerned?" Mary set her book down and looked at Elizabeth askance. "What has Mama told you?"

This was certainly something that Elizabeth had not expected. "Mama has not written to me about you," she said slowly, seeing Mary's color begin to rise. "Why? Is there something the matter?"

Mary shook her head. "No, there is nothing the matter," she answered, her voice a little higher than before.

"Then will you not simply let me know who is writing to you with such evident fervor?" Elizabeth pressed, seeing Mary's head lower. "If it is a friend or—"

"A gentleman was introduced to me at your wedding," Mary said, lifting her head and looking at Elizabeth directly. "He has been eagerly hoping that I will come to London, which I only mentioned briefly during my conversation with him since our aunt and uncle invited me to reside with them."

Elizabeth blinked rapidly, trying not to allow her surprise to show. "I see."

"I have been ignoring his letters, of course," Mary said, with a shake of her head. "It is very foolish indeed."

"Foolish?" Elizabeth repeated. "Why is it foolish? Surely—"

"Lizzie, I do not wish to speak of this any more," Mary interrupted, picking up her book. "Now, if you do not mind, I intend to get back to my reading."

Elizabeth, seeing her sister sit back and begin to read again, drew in a long breath and then rose to her feet. "Very well," she said, feeling as though she had been rather useless in speaking to both Kitty and now to Mary. "I will leave you, but if you should ever wish to speak of such a thing, you know that I am always willing to listen."

Mary said nothing and did not even glance at Elizabeth as she walked from the room. Heaving a small sigh, Elizabeth closed the door behind her and leaned against it for a moment. Just what could be wrong with *both* of her sisters?

CHAPTER 3

The following sennight was much improved from the last. Kitty was a good deal more proper and, while she did complain upon occasion, it was nothing compared to how she had been before. Mary continued to read quietly, but she also received her letters. Nothing was said to Elizabeth by either sister which, while Elizabeth found it to be a little frustrating, she was also a little relieved that the atmosphere in the house was much more pleasant.

While sitting at the dinner table one evening, the butler brought in another letter from Mrs. Bennet. Elizabeth, who had been expecting to hear from her mother, took it at once and broke open the seal, reading it quickly.

"Oh," she said slowly.

Mr. Darcy looked up at once, his hand stilling on his glass of port. "Is something wrong?"

Elizabeth shook her head, reading the letter again. "No, nothing is wrong," she said, still focused on the letter before her. She looked at Kitty, who had gone rather still, her hands under the table and the color fading from her cheeks. "Kitty,

Mama writes to tell you that Mr. Taylor—the new clergyman—has been calling for you but is disappointed that you have not been at home. She has, of course, told him that you are away for an extended duration, and this, it seems, has filled him with dismay." She glanced at Kitty, who was now staring steadfastly at her plate instead of looking directly at her. "Mary, Mother writes that she hopes you are enjoying Mr. Darcy's library."

Mary smiled and then returned to dining, whilst Kitty did not even attempt to pick up her fork. Elizabeth watched her sister carefully, and then she folded up the letter and looked towards Mr. Darcy. He, too, had noticed Kitty's reaction and was sitting quietly, watching her with sharp eyes.

"Will you have port this evening, Darcy?" Elizabeth asked, as Mr. Darcy let his gaze drift towards her. "I will take my sisters to have tea in the drawing room."

He smiled, clearly aware of what she intended. "Yes, I think I will remain here and have some port," he said, as Elizabeth rose from the table, seeing her two sisters do the same. "I will join you shortly."

Grateful for the opportunity to be alone with her sisters, Elizabeth led the way to the drawing room.

"I...I think I will retire early this evening," Kitty said quickly, before they had reached the door to the drawing room. "I am very tired and I—"

"Kitty," Elizabeth said, turning to look at her and seeing the paleness of her cheeks. "Please, come in for a few minutes at least."

It took a moment, but eventually Kitty agreed and came in with both Elizabeth and Mary. Mary, as she always did, made her way to the pianoforte and began to play a quiet piece, leaving

Elizabeth and Kitty to sit together. Elizabeth watched her sister closely, trying to find a way to encourage her to speak openly about what had been in their mother's letter.

"Mary's playing is greatly improved, is it not?" Kitty commented.

Elizabeth smiled, as Kitty settled in a chair. "Yes, it is," Elizabeth agreed quietly. "It is a joy to listen to her now."

Nothing was said for a few minutes more, and Elizabeth watched Kitty carefully. Her sister appeared to be a little more relaxed, absently watching Mary play, her hands settled quietly in her lap.

"Kitty," Elizabeth began, as gently as she could. "Might I ask you something?" She waited until Kitty's gaze returned to her. "The clergyman? Is that what you have been struggling with?"

Much to her surprise, in a single moment, Kitty's demeanor changed entirely. Her sister leaned forward, her hands over her face and a sob escaping her. Elizabeth had not known that this was such a difficulty for Kitty, and she felt herself almost at a loss as to what to do.

"Kitty," she said, as soothingly as she could, coming to sit next to her sister. "I am sorry. I did not mean to push you in speaking of this. I did not realize that it was troubling you so much."

"I...I do not know what to do!" Kitty cried, dropping her hands and looking directly at Elizabeth. "A *clergyman*, Lizzie? He is a *clergyman*!"

"But that is a very respectable profession," Elizabeth replied quickly, a little surprised that her sister had not protested about the fact that the gentleman was, in fact, calling upon her when she did not wish him to. "What else would you wish for?"

Kitty shook her head, her tears drying quickly. "But Lydia has married Mr. Wickham, has she not?"

"Yes, but Mr. Wickham is not–" Elizabeth stopped herself quickly not wanting to speak ill of Mr. Wickham, not when they were now brother and sister. "You wish to marry someone like Mr. Wickham?"

Closing her eyes, Kitty let out a long breath. "Lydia and I always spoke of the militia, of how wonderful they were. We delighted in their attentions, talked of them constantly. When Lydia married Mr. Wickham, I was glad for her, of course, but there was also some jealousy within my heart. Jealousy that she had managed to do what I had not."

Elizabeth frowned. "You wanted to marry someone from the militia?" she asked.

"That was what we *both* hoped for," Kitty explained. "But the militia have moved on now, and we do not know when they will return—and the only gentleman who seeks my company is a clergyman!"

Not quite certain what to say, Elizabeth thought quickly, trying to understand her sister's point of view but failing entirely. "Kitty, it is foolish to think of a gentleman's profession when it comes to his interest in you. What is of much greater importance is his character." She looked at Kitty steadily. "And is Mister—? Mister—?" She looked enquiringly at Kitty, obviously failing to remember the man's name.

"Mr. Taylor," Kitty filled in.

"Is Mr. Taylor a gentleman of good character?"

Kitty nodded miserably. "Yes, I believe he is. He is kind and considerate and everyone in Meryton speaks well of him."

"Then might I ask why you choose *not* to consider him?" Elizabeth asked gently. "If he is a gentleman of good character, then...?" Smiling gently at her sister, Elizabeth tried her best to be tactful, realizing that this was the very first conversation she had shared with Kitty which was of significance. Kitty had always been flighty and flippant, ignoring advice and choosing to do precisely what she and Lydia thought best. Now, however, it seemed that she was willing, at least, to consider what Elizabeth was saying.

"I do not care for him," Kitty said suddenly, lifting her chin a notch and sniffing a trifle indelicately. "Father thinks him more than suitable, of course, and has encouraged his interest, but I am determined *not* to think of him as a suitable match."

"And Mama?"

Kitty let out a bark of laughter, catching Mary's attention for a moment, the piano music hesitating before starting up again.

"You know very well what Mama is like," Kitty told Elizabeth honestly. "Now that you are wed to Mr. Darcy and Jane to Mr. Bingley, she states that a clergyman is not at all suitable for a sister-in-law of such fine gentlemen."

Elizabeth shook her head in wry amusement. "You must not listen to Mama's advice, Kitty," she told her sister firmly. "There is nothing wrong with being wed to a clergyman."

"No?" Kitty lifted one eyebrow and looked at Elizabeth pointedly. "I do not think you can criticize me should I refuse him, Lizzie, given that you yourself did not wish to marry our cousin —Mr. Collins!"

Elizabeth pressed her lips together for a moment. "I did not wish to marry Mr. Collins because he was entirely unsuitable," she said honestly. "Surely you know that!" Watching

Kitty's expression change from determination to a begrudged nodding, Elizabeth took a moment before she continued to speak. "If Mr. Collins had been likable, honest, kind, and compassionate with a true interest in me – rather than merely *deciding* that I was suitable for him after only a few minutes of thought, then I would have given him a true consideration."

Kitty bit her lip and asked, "But you would not have felt anything for him?"

"I cannot say that," Elizabeth replied honestly. "If his character had been very different, then I cannot say how I might now feel."

Tilting her head to one side, Kitty watched Elizabeth carefully for a moment. "You care for Darcy, do you not?"

"I do," replied Elizabeth, a smile overtaking her face.

"Despite his character?"

Elizabeth let out a quiet laugh. "I know that you all find it quite marvelous – quite ridiculous almost that I should find Mr. Darcy to be a most suitable gentleman, but you must be assured that I, knowing him as well as I do, find him to be just as kind and considerate as you find your Mr. Taylor."

Kitty's eyes glinted. "He is not *my* Mr. Taylor, Elizabeth," she said sternly, although there was something in her expression that told Elizabeth that there was a good deal going on within her sister's heart. "I do not think he shall ever be."

"Then you have decided against him?"

Closing her eyes, Kitty let out a long, slow breath. "It is very difficult, Lizzie. I wish to be as Lydia is, swept along with all the excitement that Mr. Wickham has brought her. And yet, there is a part of me that wants to consider Mr. Taylor, even though he is very dull indeed compared to Mr. Wickham."

A little encouraged by this, Elizabeth reached across and placed her hands over Kitty's. "There is a change with you that I have begun to see," she said gently, not wanting to upset her sister but also eager to be truthful. "Whilst it is true that Lydia married Mr. Wickham, you seem to be very willing to forget the difficulties that her marriage brought. Do you not recall the upset that ran through our family? How our father had to travel to London in order to discover them?" She saw Kitty's eyes flicker and then drop to their joined hands, clearly remembering just how distraught they had all been at the time. "Whilst Lydia *is* wed and settled, I must hope that you are not seeking the very same thing as she. I am aware that it sounded very exciting and wonderful, but it *did* bring us a great deal of difficulty."

"I am aware of that," Kitty replied, a little glumly. "And yet—"

"I understand that the desire is there," Elizabeth interrupted, not wanting to finish speaking until she had said all she now wanted to say. "I know that there is a hope that you will have the very same excitement as Lydia, but I will tell you now that my marriage, such as it is, has been just as wonderful, if not even *more* wonderful, than Lydia's whirlwind of a marriage. I can see in you a desire to improve yourself, to go with what you know would be for your best, and *that*, Kitty, is a good change."

"And the desire to step away from Mr. Taylor and to pursue someone akin to Mr. Wickham?" Kitty asked miserably.

"That is the foolish girl that you once were, when you and Lydia thought of nothing but the militia," Elizabeth answered truthfully. "Do you not feel such a change within yourself, Kitty?"

Her sister said nothing for some minutes, the piano music drifting over them both. Elizabeth waited in silence, wanting Kitty to take her time in her considerations.

"It is a battle within myself," Kitty replied, speaking with such maturity that Elizabeth wanted to clap her hands together in delight. "I feel it very strongly indeed, Lizzie. I think that is why I have been so eager to throw myself into any activity I can, for I want nothing more than to forget what our father has said and the look on Mr. Taylor's face when he comes to greet me." She closed her eyes, but Elizabeth could not help but smile. This Mr. Taylor appeared to be quite taken with Kitty, and Kitty, she was sure, was well aware of it.

"I am glad you have spoken to me about him," Elizabeth told her sister, lifting her hand from Kitty's. "I think I should like to meet this Mr. Taylor and to see just how eager he is to be in your company!" Laughing, she caught Kitty's red face and self-conscious smile. "Continue to consider things carefully, Kitty, and come to speak to me whenever you wish it. Although, I will state that you cannot simply run away from Longbourn and from Mr. Taylor." She rose, as the maid walked in with a tray set for tea. "That will never bring you satisfaction."

CHAPTER 4

"Elizabeth?" a male voice called out.

Elizabeth looked up at once, knowing that the only person who called her by such a name was her dear husband.

"Yes, Darcy?" she asked, rising out of her seat, only for Mr. Darcy to wave a hand and encourage her to sit back down again. "Is there something the matter?"

Mr. Darcy shook his head. "No, indeed, there is nothing wrong in the least," he said, reassuring her at once. "It is only that I have received a letter from Georgiana."

Elizabeth's face lit up. "Georgiana? Is she to return home soon?"

Mr. Darcy smiled fondly back at her. "I am blessed to know that my wife cares for my sister so deeply," he said, coming towards her and holding out his hand – which Elizabeth gave to him almost at once. "You are loveliness itself, my dear."

Despite this being her husband, despite the fact she heard such accolades very regularly, Elizabeth still felt herself blush, as he lifted her hand to his mouth and kissed the back of it. The look in his eyes made her heart swell with love, her joy growing steadily.

"Mr. and Mrs. Reacher have been very glad to have her," he said, referring to the friends of his family, who had offered to take Georgiana for an extended visit in London during Mr. Darcy and Elizabeth's honeymoon. "They state there is no urgency for me to come collect her, and they also wanted to assure me that they are more than delighted to have her for a little longer."

"That is very kind of them," Elizabeth replied with a warm smile. "Although I should be glad to see her again."

Darcy nodded, a small frown flickering between his brows. "I wonder, then, how your sisters would feel about a trip to London?" he asked, looking at Elizabeth carefully. "Would they appreciate such a thing? Would they wish to go with us? Or would they rather return to Longbourn?"

Elizabeth hesitated. "I do not think that there will be a good deal of protest about going to London," she said, thinking quickly. "Kitty will be very glad to go, I am sure." She was considering how London would be further away still from Mr. Taylor, which Kitty would certainly be eager for.

"And Mary?"

Biting her lip for a moment, Elizabeth lifted one shoulder. "She may protest, but your townhouse in London also has a pianoforte and an extensive library, does it not?"

He chuckled. "Indeed, it does!" he replied, letting go of her hand and looking down at his letter. "Then I shall write to them this afternoon and tell them that we hope to be in London within the next week. Georgiana can remove to the townhouse, and we shall enjoy a few days in London before we return to Pemberley."

Elizabeth felt a spiral of excitement burning through her. "I think that is a wonderful idea, Darcy," she told him, seeing him smile. "I am very much looking forward to seeing Georgiana again, whether in London or in Pemberley itself.

A frown slid from Mr. Darcy's face. "We shall have to ensure your mother is informed of our intention to travel with your sisters," he said, a little frustrated. "No doubt she will want to know *precisely* where we are and how long we will be there."

"You may find her in London ready to meet us!" Elizabeth replied, teasing him and causing Mr. Darcy's eyes to widened for a moment. Rising, she kissed him lightly. "Now, you write your letter to Georgiana, and I shall inform Kitty and Mary and see whether they wish to join us." She laughed, as she walked to the door. "Although I am quite certain neither of them shall refuse!"

~

Kitty, however, was nowhere to be found. Elizabeth wondered if she had gone to take a walk in the grounds. Instead of going in search of her, Elizabeth went in search of Mary, who was much easier to find, given that she was, yet again, in the library.

"Mary?" Elizabeth walked inside, making sure to keep her voice and her steps quiet so as not to intrude too much. Seeing her sister's inquisitive look, she sat down opposite her. "There is something I have to speak to about, but I would be happy to wait until you are finished reading."

Mary considered, then shook her head, setting the book down carefully so that it still remained open in its place. "I should only rush through the words, given that you are here, rather than concentrate on them as I ought," she said with a pained sigh. "What is it that you must so urgently speak to me about?"

Elizabeth wondered if she ought to begin by informing Mary that the library at Darcy's townhouse in London would be just as suitable as this one, given that she was clearly only interested in continuing her own personal study.

"Mr. Darcy has suggested that we take a short trip to London," she said, with as much delight as she could muster. "The townhouse there has its own library, of course, and I am sure that you will be able to continue your reading there."

Mary said nothing, her fingers tightening together as she held them in her lap.

"It is because Georgiana, who is with a family friend, is more than ready to return to Pemberley," Elizabeth continued, wondering at Mary's silence. "Mr. Darcy thought it would be enjoyable for us all to visit London, since I know that you have never been there yourself."

Mary looked away suddenly, a tight breath escaping from her.

"Mary?" Elizabeth queried, feeling a little confused. "Is there something the matter? You do not wish to go to London perhaps?"

Looking back at Elizabeth, Mary's lips remained in a thin line. "Of course I should like to go," she said tightly. "You are quite correct. I have never been to London."

Elizabeth, who was not at all certain that she believed this, regarded her sister with a sharp eye, which, it seemed, Mary was well aware of. Turning her head to one side, Mary made to pick up her book, but Elizabeth stayed her hand with a single word.

"Mary."

With a heavy sigh and a resigned expression, Mary looked back at Elizabeth. "Yes, my dear sister?"

"I know there is something that you are unwilling to share with me," Elizabeth said firmly, feeling a sense of responsibility for Mary. "I presume that this has something to do with the letters you have been receiving?" She held Mary's gaze steadily. "Do these letters come from someone in London?"

It had been a mere presumption, but from the way that heat began to infuse Mary's cheeks, as well as the widening of her eyes, Elizabeth realized – with a sense of satisfaction – that she had come close to the truth.

"Mary," she continued gently when her sister said nothing. "Will you not tell me the truth?" Suddenly recalling all of Lydia's foolish behavior, Elizabeth's chest tightened for a moment, although her mind told her that Mary would never behave in a similar fashion. "If we are to go to London, I must insist that you tell me about these letters."

Mary closed her eyes, her book now entirely forgotten. "Th-There is nothing specific to tell, Lizzie," she said, although the faltering in her voice did not speak of conviction. "I have been receiving letters from a particular gentleman who resides in London. He very much wishes me to call upon him, stating that he has a Muzio Clementi pianoforte, which, he believes, is one of the best to have ever been built."

Elizabeth tilted her head. "That is a very generous offer, Mary," she said, trying to hide her astonishment that Darcy, it seemed, had been proven correct in his suggestion that Mary might have some sort of admirer. "Am I correct in presuming that each of these letters has been encouraging you to find a way to come to London?"

Letting out a huff of breath, Mary looked away. "It is nothing more than foolishness," she said, clearly trying to brush away any suggestion that there was any more to it than that. "He wishes me to come; I wish to remain...far from him."

Elizabeth considered this carefully, not quite certain whether what Mary said was the truth. She did not know Mary particularly well, for Mary had always kept her thoughts and feelings on *certain* matters to herself. She was always ready to express her considerations in judgement on her sisters' behavior, and Elizabeth had certainly never expected that Mary would be pursued by *any* gentleman – or that she, in return, would allow herself to consider them. There was not a gentleman around who would reach her particular standards.

"Might I enquire as to his age?"

Mary waved a hand and said, "That is irrelevant."

"All the same, I should like to know."

Mary sighed heavily again, as though Elizabeth's questions were heavy upon her. "He is one and thirty."

A little surprised, Elizabeth allowed herself a small nod. "I see. And what is his profession?"

Mary lifted one shoulder, as if to state that such a thing was of little interest to her. "He is a clerk, Lizzie. Nothing more than a simple clerk."

Rather surprised to hear that a clerk should have such an instrument as the one Mary had described, Elizabeth frowned heavily. "I see."

"The piano is the only thing of value he owns," Mary replied with a sigh. "A gift, I believe, to his sister on the day of her wedding from her new husband. She married very well indeed, but they both sadly passed from this world to the next not long after their marriage."

"That must have been very difficult for him," Elizabeth replied, thinking silently to herself that Mary had either spoken to this particular gentleman at length or read each and every one of his letters. "And a clerk is not a profession to be ashamed of, Mary."

Mary lifted one eyebrow and said, "It is not to Mama's standards."

"But you must not listen to Mama," Elizabeth replied swiftly. "If you are willing to consider this gentleman, then why not do so?"

Mary closed her eyes again. "You sound very much like our dear uncle, Lizzie," she told her. "Mr. Phillips states that Mr. Reid is quite suitable and is eager for me to consider him further."

"Our uncle?" Elizabeth repeated, rather confused. "Why should our uncle seek to have you consider Mr. Reid?"

Letting out an exasperated breath, Mary opened her eyes. "Because Mr. Reid is our uncle's clerk," she said, as though Elizabeth ought to have known such a thing already. "That is why."

Elizabeth held back her surprise with an effort. Murmuring that she understood, she sat back in her chair and regarded Mary closely. Both Mary and Kitty had mentioned their mother, Mrs. Bennet, whom Elizabeth knew would be pushing them both from their particular gentleman merely because the men did not suit her intentions.

"And might I ask why *you* are so unwilling to consider him?" she asked, her voice laced with caution. "There appears to be some sort of recalcitrance on your part."

Mary arched one eyebrow, no hint of color in her cheeks or any other indication that she actually thought well of Mr. Reid. "I have never truly considered matrimony, Lizzie," she said slowly. "Our mother has always been eager to point out my lack of beauty compared to my sisters, and certainly, I have been well aware of the severe lack of interest from any gentleman of our acquaintance."

"You mean to say that you had not expected such a thing and thus are now a little confused?" Elizabeth ventured, a little uncertain as to what Mary meant. "Or that you have no intention of considering him at all?"

Her sister did not immediately answer. Instead, she had a faraway look in her eyes.

"As yet, Lizzie," she said eventually, "I am a little uncertain. I have not replied to any of Mr. Reid's letters, but he insists on writing to me regardless." A slight twist to her lips betrayed her frustrations. "I shall come to London, of course, but do not press me into returning a note to Mr. Reid, or to attempt to see him."

Feeling a little relieved that she now knew the truth of Kitty and Mary's circumstances, Elizabeth rose to her feet. "I quite understand," she answered with honesty. "But I should like you to be free to talk to me whenever you wish."

"That is kind of you," Mary answered graciously. "But I do not see that there is anything particular to talk of."

Elizabeth wanted to respond by saying that there was a very good deal to speak about, but not wanting to press her sister further, she merely smiled and reached out to press Mary's shoulder.

"Well, if such a thing should change," she reminded Mary, "then you know that I am here to listen and to offer advice where I can."

Mary nodded, turned her head, and picked up her book again. It seemed that, for the time being at least, this conversation was finished.

~

"I cannot quite believe it, Darcy!" exclaimed Elizabeth.

Mr. Darcy tipped up Elizabeth's chin with a gentle finger, his eyes dancing as the sun shone brightly all around them. "Can you not?"

Elizabeth shook her head at her husband's teasing, as a gentle breeze lifted some of her curls from around her temples. "You know very well that it is *most* extraordinary for Mary to have a potential suitor, given that she has shunned all such things before and certainly has made no attempt to garner any interest from anyone."

"But she still shuns the idea now, does she not?"

Hesitating, Elizabeth chose her words carefully. "There is certainly a reluctance, yes, but I cannot tell if it comes from a lack of willingness on her part or a lack of experience in such matters."

Mr. Darcy chuckled, slipped his arm about Elizabeth's waist, and began to walk with her through the beautiful gardens of Pemberley. "At least you reacted well to what she told you," he said with a smile. "Although it appears that she will not need any further assistance!"

"So she has said," Elizabeth answered with a sigh. "And as for Kitty – I find myself quite at a loss as to what I should do. I believe that *her* reluctance comes from a struggle between her past behavior and the new character that is now beginning to form."

Considering this, Mr. Darcy took a moment before he replied. "I think that all change within one's character takes time," he said, with a knowing look. "You were able to distinguish that when it came to my own character, were you not?"

Elizabeth smiled gently, looking up at her husband. "Indeed. As well as within myself, I suppose. I saw my faults for what they were."

"And thus, a change was made," Mr. Darcy replied, pulling her a little closer as they walked. "With Kitty, I believe that she will simply need a little more time before the choice no longer becomes as difficult or as pronounced as it is at present. I am quite certain that, in good company such as yours, her change will continue to take place and she will soon decide what is best."

"I must hope so," Elizabeth replied. "I do think that this clergyman, whoever he is, will be more than suitable for Kitty – although he would have been considered much too sensible and staid by her some months ago!"

Mr. Darcy lifted his brows. "That in itself is a good change, is it not?" he said. "Although, given that your mother will not approve of him, will that not hinder Kitty somewhat?"

"It may," Elizabeth answered, knowing that there was much truth to her statement. "She does not think well of Mary's gentleman either, but Mary, of course, does not set great store by Mama's opinions."

Stopping for a moment, Mr. Darcy turned to face Elizabeth, and as she looked up into his eyes, she felt her heart quicken at the love she could see in their depth.

"It seems then, that our trip to London might become a little more exciting than I had first thought," he said, making Elizabeth laugh. "Perhaps, by our return, we will have not one but *two* sisters ready to find themselves quite happily engaged!"

"I can barely allow myself to think so," Elizabeth replied, before reaching up to kiss him.

CHAPTER 5

As the carriage rolled into London, Elizabeth could not help but catch her breath at the unfamiliar sights and sounds that came with being in the city. Her two sisters were equally entranced, although Mary, she could tell, was doing all she could to pretend that she did not give any consideration to being in town. Even so, her eyes continued to stray towards the carriage window, and Elizabeth smiled to herself, knowing full well that London itself would capture any heart and mind, even one as determined as Mary's.

"Darcy's townhouse is not far," Elizabeth said, recalling the house with fondness. She had only been in it once before, when they had been returning from their honeymoon, but the few days she had spent there had been very happy days indeed. "London has many delights, I must say, but it is important not to become overwhelmed." Looking sharply at Kitty, she saw her sister glance back at her, clearly aware that Elizabeth was referring to her.

"I am sure there will be many delights here," Mary murmured, her eyes still tugging towards the view outside. "But I shall enjoy my time in Mr. Darcy's library, as I have been doing before."

"I highly doubt that," Kitty replied, with a note of sarcasm in her voice. "You shall be just as willing as I to go and explore, I am sure, no matter how hard you try to hide such eagerness."

Mary opened her mouth to argue, but Elizabeth – wearied as she was from her journey and from her sisters' conversation – broke in before she could do so.

"Mary, you will find many things here to please you," Elizabeth said firmly. "Bookshops, perhaps? And London has a few magnificent museums, which I am sure will prove to be most entertaining."

Despite the fact that no smile pulled Mary's lips, there came a flicker of excitement in her eyes that made Elizabeth chuckle. "And as for you, Kitty," she continued, turning to her other sister. "There will be plenty of shops for you to find new ribbons and the like. Mayhap even a new bonnet?"

This seemed to be a thoroughly wonderful idea to Kitty, who clapped her hands together, evidently forgetting entirely about her harsh words to Mary. Thankfully, within a few minutes, the carriage came to a stop, relieving Elizabeth of the need to continue any conversation with either of her sisters. Mr. Darcy, who had been riding ahead on his stallion, now stood waiting for them at the front door of the house, his expression brightening as Elizabeth climbed out of the carriage.

"My dear," he said warmly, reaching to catch her hands in his as she reached the top of the steps. "How was the journey?" His eyes darted to Mary and Kitty, who were only now beginning to climb the steps. "I do hope you are not overly fatigued."

Elizabeth allowed herself a quiet laugh. "Not overly, no", she answered, pressing his hands. "Although I am relieved to be here at last."

Turning, she pressed her hand through Mr. Darcy's arm and walked inside, with both Kitty and Mary following behind. Her mind filled with memories of the last time she had been within this house, and she let out a contented sigh, which made Mr. Darcy smile down at her.

"You are glad to be here, I think."

She looked up at him and smiled. "Yes, very glad indeed," she replied. "Although I am sure that, within a few days, I shall begin to miss Pemberley and the beautiful grounds that bring me so much joy."

Mr. Darcy laughed and pulled her a little closer. "I am glad that you find so much joy in our home," he said, sending a warmth to her heart as he referred to it as "our" home. "We shall return to Pemberley soon enough." Coming to a stop, he turned and snapped his heels together. "Catherine," he said, using Kitty's formal name, "and Mary. I do hope that this house pleases you."

The two ladies nodded together, their eyes roving around the large hallway for a moment before returning to Mr. Darcy.

"Georgiana will be dining with us this evening," he continued, making Elizabeth brighten at the news. "And tomorrow, we shall attend an evening assembly."

Kitty gasped, her eyes wide with delight and her hands at her mouth. Mary, however, did not react in any way other than for sudden glimmer to come into her eyes.

"How wonderful!" Kitty exclaimed, sounding utterly delighted and a little terrified in equal measure. "But what shall I wear?"

She looked desperately at Elizabeth. "Do you think I have anything suitable?"

Before Elizabeth could answer, Mr. Darcy cleared his throat, drawing Kitty's attention. "I should be very glad, Catherine, if you would go into town tomorrow with Mary, in order to purchase a new gown. One for each of you, I mean." He squeezed Elizabeth's hand. "And for you also, my dear, if you should wish it."

Elizabeth felt her heart overflow with the love that filled her heart. Mr. Darcy could be so very generous, and now, here he was, expressing that same generosity of heart towards her two sisters.

Mary replied, "That is very kind of you, sir, but I should not—"

But before she could finish her thought, she was silenced by a sharp nudge from Kitty. Elizabeth looked at her sister sharply, and Mary bowed her head, murmuring only a "thank you" instead of anything more. It would not do, Elizabeth knew, for her sister to refuse such generosity – not when Mr. Darcy was being as kind as he was.

"Then it is all settled," Mr. Darcy said, clearly satisfied by the response. "Tomorrow, into town you shall go!"

Kitty let out a squeal of delight, which she tempered after only a moment. Mary said nothing more, her cheeks a little red as she kept her gaze low.

"I will show you to your rooms," Elizabeth said, stepping forward. "There will be a little time to rest before changing for dinner." Throwing back a grateful glance towards her husband, she turned to lead her sisters to the staircase, more glad than ever that they had found such a happiness together despite all the trouble that had gone before.

~

"It is really quite delightful to be back with you again," said Elizabeth, as she smiled warmly at her sister-in-law.

She started thinking to herself that Georgiana was a little changed since she had last seen her. There was certainly a serenity about her countenance, but mayhap it came from a joy that was deep within her heart to be back, reunited with her brother at last.

"You had an excellent time with your friends, I understand," Elizabeth said, as Georgiana nodded. "I hope you will not be too disappointed to be with us again!"

Georgiana laughed, making Kitty smile. "Indeed not, I am very glad to be back with you all. Although," she continued, looking at Elizabeth, "I confess that it might take a little time to become used to being in Pemberley again, with things a little... changed." A slight flush touched her cheeks, and she looked at Elizabeth for what Elizabeth presumed was a little reassurance.

"There is nothing you need worry about," Elizabeth replied firmly. "I confess that it has taken me some time also to become used to living in Pemberley, although it is quite magnificent." She smiled fondly at Mr. Darcy. "I find myself quite astonished that I still have such a wonderful home and husband."

All was quiet for a moment as Mr. Darcy looked back at her, his expression filled with a gentle sweetness that spoke to her heart.

"I must hope that I shall soon find a similar situation to your own," Georgiana murmured, after a long moment. "I confess that I—"

"There is no urgency for such a thing," Mr. Darcy interrupted. "None whatsoever, Georgiana. Pemberley is still your home. Nothing has changed for you, I assure you."

"Indeed," Elizabeth agreed, thinking that whilst it was good for Georgiana to at least be considering such a thing, there was no need for her to feel pushed from her home simply because Elizabeth was now wed to Mr. Darcy. "Now, are you to attend the evening assembly with us tomorrow?"

"I am!" Georgiana exclaimed, immediately distracted from her discussion. "As is, I believe, your aunt and uncle, Elizabeth."

"Oh?"

It was not Elizabeth who made this exclamation but Mary. Elizabeth turned her head to look at her sister, seeing the color begin to pull from Mary's cheeks.

"Mr. and Mrs. Phillips, of course," Georgiana replied, with a smile towards her brother. "I know Sir Dalton, of course, and was easily able to ensure they were given an invitation." A small flicker of doubt climbed into her eyes. "I do hope I did not overstep or do wrong, brother. I thought only of Lizzie and her delight at seeing them again."

Mr. Darcy laughed, reached across the table, and pressed his sister's hand. "You need not look so anxious, my dear sister," he told her firmly. "I am sure Catherine, Mary, *and* Lizzie will be more than delighted to see their uncle and aunt again."

"We shall be *very* glad to see them again," Kitty said, beaming at Georgiana. "That was very kind of you to consider us in such a way, Georgiana."

"Very kind," Mary echoed, although she did not look anywhere near as pleased as Kitty. Elizabeth watched her with interest, wondering if Mary was anxious about meeting her aunt and uncle again for fear that they would tell Mr. Reid that she was now in London.

She caught Mr. Darcy watching her and smiled back at him, one eyebrow lifting slightly as he glanced towards Mary. With a small nod, Elizabeth returned the conversation to something other than the evening assembly, wondering when she would be able to speak to Mary further about this Mr. Reid, who seemed to have such a strange effect upon her sister.

~

"That gown is quite lovely on you, Kitty," Elizabeth commented.

Kitty whirled around, the beautiful, light blue gown spreading out around her. A delighted giggle came from her as she clapped her hands together, beaming delightedly at Elizabeth.

"Do you think it will do for this evening, Georgiana?" she asked, her eyes dancing as Georgiana laughed. "Do you think I will look well in this?"

"You look very lovely indeed," Georgiana replied, her gown for this evening already chosen. "Now, Mary, where are you?"

Elizabeth smiled to herself as a heavy sigh came from behind Kitty. Mary had changed into a gown that Elizabeth practically had to force her into. She had refused to even consider a new gown until Elizabeth had reminded her, in no uncertain terms, that it would be very rude to refuse Mr. Darcy's great generosity and kindness. That had forced Mary's hand, for she had not wanted to behave in such a way, but she had still given very little attention to the types of gowns offered to her. Elizabeth had, therefore, chosen the gown that she had considered to be the most suitable for Mary's coloring, and thus, Mary now stood clad in a gown of light pink, which, thankfully, took some of Mary's paleness from her cheeks.

The only issue, however, was that Mary now looked quite miserable. There was not a smile on her face, no joy in her expression and no brightness in her eyes. All in all, she looked as though she were about to attend some sort of torturous event rather than a joyous evening assembly.

"Lovely," Elizabeth said, forcing a smile, as Mary shook her head and looked away. "That color is very good on you, Mary."

Mary sniffed but said nothing.

"I am sure you shall garner a good deal of attention," Georgiana continued, her voice filled with enthusiasm. "There will be dancing this evening, and I am certain that—"

"I am not certain that I shall consider dancing," Mary interrupted. "It is not the sort of entertainment that I enjoy."

Kitty laughed, a slight twist in her voice. "Mary, you will have to at least *pretend* to enjoy this evening," she said, turning away from her sister in evident frustration. "It is very kind of Sir Dalton to consider inviting us."

Mary let out a long breath and lifted her chin, and then a tiny smile lifted the corner of her mouth. "I see," she said. "I shall behave properly, of course."

Grateful that, whilst Mary's behavior could be frustrating at times, her sense of propriety would remain constant, Elizabeth nodded serenely. "Then it appears we have all the gowns we require." Gesturing to Kitty, she sent her back beside Mary. "If you would change, then we can return to the townhouse."

With Mary and Kitty both hurrying to change, Elizabeth led Georgiana back into the shop, speaking quietly with the dressmaker for a few moments. She did not notice a man coming into the shop, although he came to stand near to the dressmaker, ready to speak to her thereafter.

"I believe you have a hat waiting for me," he said, as Elizabeth turned away, so as to give the fellow space to speak to the dressmaker undisturbed. "It is under the name of Mr. Taylor."

The name struck Elizabeth as someone she knew, but she dismissed the idea rather quickly, reminding herself that there would be a good many "Mr. Taylors" in London. She and Georgiana kept a conversation flowing about the evening that would soon follow, but it was not until Kitty and Mary emerged again that Elizabeth suddenly recalled where she had known that name before.

"The dresses will be sent to the address you have supplied, Mrs. Darcy," the dressmaker said, as she began to lift various boxes onto the counter. "Now, if there is anything else that you might wish to purchase?" She indicated a shelf, which had ribbons laid out upon it, and another which held beautiful silk gloves. Elizabeth was about to state that they had all that they needed, only to hear Kitty speak.

"M-Mr. Taylor?"

She turned around slowly, astonished to see the gentleman who had walked into the shop staring, wide eyed, at Kitty, the color rushing to his cheeks.

"Good afternoon, Miss Bennet," the gentleman said, managing to speak clearly despite his obvious astonishment. "I did not expect to see you in London. I thought you were with your sister in—"

"We came to London to stay in Mr. Darcy's townhouse for a short time," Kitty replied, her voice unnaturally high. "Might I enquire as to why you are in London?"

Mr. Taylor cleared his throat, glancing towards Elizabeth and Mary, before looking to Georgiana, clearly aware that introductions had not been made. "I-I am with my elder brother," he said, shuffling his feet a little awkwardly. "Only for a short respite, you understand. I cannot leave my parishioners for long." His smile was a little tentative.

"I see," Kitty said, dropping her head before finally catching Elizabeth's eye. "I see. Oh, do forgive me, Mr. Taylor." Her own cheeks hot, she finally introduced first Elizabeth, then Mary, and finally Georgiana. Mr. Taylor nodded and bowed to each of them in turn, his behavior quite impeccable. Elizabeth found herself considering him more than respectable, and certainly, from the expression on Kitty's face, having a rather interesting effect on her sister.

"It is very good to meet you, Mr. Taylor," Elizabeth said, catching Kitty's urgent look. "We are to be entertained this evening at an assembly, but perhaps you would like to call tomorrow? I am sure we would be very glad to see you."

This appeared to be the wrong suggestion, given Kitty's wide eyes, but Elizabeth merely smiled and received Mr. Taylor's eager words of thanks and acceptance with a nod of her head.

"Until tomorrow then, Mr. Taylor," she said firmly, as Kitty bobbed a quick curtsy. "I look forward to introducing you to my husband, Mr. Darcy."

"I thank you, Mrs. Darcy," Mr. Taylor said before bowing and, with a final glance towards Kitty, taking his leave of them all.

CHAPTER 6

"I do not understand why you had to suggest such a thing, Lizzie!"

Elizabeth let out a long, controlled breath. Kitty had been very quiet on their return to the house, but thereafter, she had broken into loud complaint, which, even at the evening assembly, still continued on.

"Kitty, do stop being foolish," Elizabeth said firmly. "I did what was expected. It would have been rude to leave him standing there without inviting him to take tea with us or some other such thing."

Kitty let out a long, exasperated breath, shaking her head. "I do not want him to visit us."

"But why ever not?" Elizabeth asked, as gently as she could. "He appears to be a very amiable gentleman, and I cannot understand why you should not wish to have him in your company."

Kitty said nothing, her eyes darting all around the room rather than saying anything at all to Elizabeth. Watching her carefully, Elizabeth felt her heart squeeze with sympathy. Her sister was clearly troubled over this gentleman, and although she wanted her desperately to do choose the correct path, Elizabeth knew she could not force her to do so.

"I did not expect to see him here," Kitty mumbled, folding her gloved hands over her chest. "It was something of a shock, I will confess."

"He appears to be quite taken with you," Elizabeth said, as gently as she could. "Whilst he was certainly as surprised as you were, there was a delight in his eyes that he could not hide."

Shaking her head furiously, Kitty looked up at Elizabeth with an almost mutinous gaze. "I could not be the wife of a clergyman, Lizzie!" she exclaimed, looking rather frustrated. "It is not at all what I thought I should be."

Elizabeth chose her words carefully, although she felt a deep irritation for the many, *many* times Mrs. Bennet had suggested that her girls were meant to marry the most excellent of gentlemen. "That does not matter," she said carefully. "To be truthful, I never once thought I should marry someone such as Mr. Darcy, but it appears that I—"

"But Mr. Darcy is rich!" Kitty protested, throwing up her hands. "He is wealthy with a wonderful estate, and you have all that you require!"

"Those things are not what I sought, Kitty," Elizabeth quickly answered. "They are superfluous."

Shaking her head, Kitty planted her hands on her hips. "But you are now very well situated, Lizzie! I should also be able to find a suitable gentleman, who is wealthy enough to keep me content, as well as, perhaps, stirring my affections."

Elizabeth sighed and turned her attention away from her sister for a moment or two, trying to keep her composure. No matter what she said, Kitty was still determined to find a handsome and wealthy gentleman—just as she and Jane had done—instead of considering the sort of gentleman who might be more than suitable for her. Mr. Taylor, for example.

Whilst Elizabeth had to admit that she did find it a little difficult to imagine Kitty as the wife of a clergyman, should her sister continue to leave her silliness and immaturity behind as she had been, then there was no reason why she could not be.

"I do *like* Mr. Taylor." Kitty's voice was so soft that Elizabeth had to struggle to hear her, trying desperately to hide her surprise that Kitty had spoken so openly. "But still, I find myself pulling away. I remember Mama's voice, telling me that I could do a good deal better than a mere clergyman."

Closing her eyes, Elizabeth chose her words with care. "It is not Mama's voice that you need to listen to, Kitty," she said, opening her eyes to see her sister's eyes widen just a little, her expression more open than it had been before. "Nor, in fact, is it mine." Smiling, she reached out and pressed Kitty's hand. "It is only to your own voice that you must listen. Consider carefully and decide what it is that you *truly* want."

Letting go of Kitty's hand and seeing Georgiana approaching, ready to speak to Kitty, Elizabeth quickly took her leave. Looking around the room for any sign of Mary, she quickly spotted her sister talking to her aunt, Mrs. Phillips. With a bright smile of welcome on her face, Mrs. Phillips held out her hands towards Elizabeth, greeting her with a warm embrace as she came forward.

"How *very* good to see you again, Lizzie!" Mrs. Phillips cried, looking at Elizabeth with a delighted smile stretching across her face. "I have been so looking forward to seeing you again."

"And I, you," Elizabeth replied, pressing her aunt's hands. "How are you both?"

Mrs. Phillips laughed. "Very well indeed," she said and smiled, throwing a quick look towards Mary. "Your uncle will be glad to see you also, I am sure." Tilting her head, she regarded Elizabeth carefully. "You look very well, my dear. I believe marriage suits you!"

"It does indeed," Elizabeth replied, honestly. "I have found the first few months living in Pemberley to be utterly delightful." Her expression softened. "And Mr. Darcy is a very kind and attentive husband."

Mrs. Phillips looked very pleased to hear this news. "Then we must hope that, very soon, your sister will find an equally attentive and kind husband." Her gaze slid to Mary, and Elizabeth immediately saw Mary blush and drop her head.

"This is your husband's clerk, I believe," Elizabeth said, not wanting to embarrass Mary further, but knowing that she could not pretend she knew nothing. "Is he in London at present?"

Clapping her hands together, Mrs. Phillips eyes seemed to glow with excitement. "Indeed, he is," she said, as though Mary ought to be thoroughly delighted at such news. "I have already informed him, of course, that Mary is now in London, and he has asked permission to write to her here." One eyebrow lifted as she looked from Elizabeth to Mary and back again.

Struggling to answer, Elizabeth glanced at Mary, wondering what her sister would prefer. Mary had never been open with her emotions, unwilling to express precisely what she felt, and thus it meant that Elizabeth was in something of a bind. To say that such a thing would be more than acceptable when Mary did not wish it, would put herself and Mary at odds. To refuse when Mary might, perhaps, desire to continue to receive such letters—despite all appearances—could upset matters further.

"It is not for I to say whether or not such a thing can continue," Elizabeth said, after a few moments. "Mary, what is it you desire?" The question was direct and straight to the point, but perhaps, Elizabeth considered, that was for the best. Mary was often forthcoming with her declarations on others, to state, quite clearly what she believed was wrong or improper, so mayhap she would be just as forthcoming with what she thought on this particular matter.

Mary, however, did not give as instantaneous a response as Elizabeth had hoped. Instead, she opened her mouth and closed it again multiple times, looking helplessly from Mrs. Phillips to Elizabeth and back again, her fingers twisting together tightly. Elizabeth had never seen her in such a state before, realizing that Mary was feeling so much emotion, so much that she had never experienced in her life before, that she was quite unable to make a decision.

"You do not know," Mrs. Phillips said kindly, seeing Mary's distress. "Might I suggest that you allow him to write to you, Mary? It would be better, I think, than asking him to call upon you!"

Color faded from Mary's cheeks. "I should not like that," she answered, her voice barely loud enough for Elizabeth to hear. "Not yet, certainly."

Elizabeth nodded kindly, putting her hand to Mary's arm. "That is wise, Mary," she said, her voice gentle. "But if you enjoy his letters – and you need not admit to me that you do – then why not permit him to continue writing?"

Mary closed her eyes tightly and then nodded her head, her hands folded across her arms. "Yes, I..." Lifting her chin, she took in a deep breath, appearing a little more resolute. "Yes, Aunt Phillips, I would be glad for his letters to continue. For the time being, of course."

"Of course," Mrs. Phillips replied, with a gentle expression. "I know that Mr. Reid will be very glad to hear that you are willing to continue receiving his letters."

Mary murmured something incoherent, only for a gentleman to come near to them and request Mary's company for a dance. Elizabeth, who did not know the man, made to protest, but Mrs. Phillips quietened her with a squeeze of her arm. Much to Elizabeth's astonishment, Mary hesitated for only a moment before accepting. Utterly astonished, Elizabeth watched with wide eyes as Mary was led to the dance floor.

"Good gracious, Aunt!" Elizabeth exclaimed. "Is this your influence?"

Mrs. Phillips laughed, her eyes twinkling. "That gentleman is Mr. Bridgeford, who is a very kind fellow with an excellent character." She smiled fondly at her niece. "I introduced them both earlier, but I certainly did not expect Mary to accept his request to dance!"

"Nor did I," Elizabeth murmured, still watching Mary with a surprised gaze. "But perhaps Mary is changing just a little."

"As is Kitty," Mrs. Phillips remarked, gesturing towards Kitty, who was talking to a lady and a gentleman that Elizabeth had been introduced to only a short time ago. There was no foolish smile on her face, no ridiculous laughter escaping her. Rather, she appeared to be quite at her ease, speaking well and behaving with such propriety that Elizabeth could not help but smile.

"Kitty, I think – if I may be so bold as to speak without restraint – is doing very well indeed...now that she is far from Lydia's side."

"And from your mother's, as dear as she is to me," Mrs. Phillips added, with a knowing look in her eye. "You know that you need not pretend with me, Lizzie." With a slightly lifted brow, she studied Elizabeth's face. "Do you fear her returning to Longbourn?"

Elizabeth hesitated, knowing that she could speak openly with her aunt and also wanting to ensure she spoke honestly. "Kitty has a gentleman interested in her also, Aunt Phillips. In fact, he is here in London at this very moment, although we did not know it until earlier today!"

Mrs. Phillips' expression lit up. "Indeed? And is he sensible?"

Laughing, Elizabeth nodded. "Very," she told her. "In fact, he is a clergyman. But, of course," she continued, seeing Mrs. Phillips wide-eyed expression, "Mama does not think him suitable for Kitty."

Understanding flared in her aunt's eyes. "Because she believes that her remaining daughters can marry someone with the same wealth as Mr. Darcy and Mr. Bingley?"

Glad that her aunt understood so much without her having to explain, Elizabeth nodded. "That is quite what Mama believes, yes," she said, softly. "I believe that Kitty has begun to care for this particular gentleman but is struggling against the words of Mama and her own prior hopes."

"You mean to say that she believes a clergyman is not the sort of gentleman she had ever imagined marrying," Aunt Phillips said, with a gleam in her eye. "Which I quite understand. To be truthful, I myself would never have suggested that Kitty would make an excellent clergyman's wife, but if her character is changing, as you have suggested..." Trailing off, she looked questioningly at Elizabeth.

Letting out a small sigh, Elizabeth smiled ruefully at her aunt. "I felt the same as you, Aunt," she confessed. "To be truthful, at times, I still cannot quite consider Kitty as the wife of a clergyman, but to see how she is changing, to see the way that her character is developing into that of a mature, proper young lady, I confess that now I might be able to see her in such a position."

"So you encourage the match?"

Elizabeth lifted one shoulder in a half-hearted shrug. "I do not encourage her to choose him, no. Rather, I encourage her to consider her feelings and to do what will bring her happiness. Although," she continued, with a half-smile, "I have certainly reminded her, on more than one occasion, that being a clergyman does not make him any less worthy of her than a gentleman with a great fortune. I have tried to impress upon her that such things as wealth and grandeur matter very little. If one's husband can support both himself and his wife in a satisfactory manner for the rest of his days, then that should be more than enough for a lady."

Mrs. Phillips nodded sagely. "That is very wise advice indeed, Lizzie."

"And, of course, Mr. Darcy and I should be glad to help Kitty, should she ever be in difficulty," Elizabeth finished. "Although I have not said such a thing to her as yet." She made to smile, only for a sudden feeling to grip her. Blinking rapidly, she put one hand out to Mrs. Phillips, feeling a dizziness wash over her.

"Goodness, Lizzie, are you quite all right?"

The moment passed rather quickly, but it left Elizabeth feeling rather weak, her hand still clinging to her aunt's arm.

"I think I should sit down," she said, a little quietly, only for a strong arm to come around her waist.

"My dear." Mr. Darcy's voice was gruff, betraying his concern. "From across the room, I saw you swaying and gripping Mrs. Phillips' arm." Looking into her eyes, he frowned hard. "You are unwell."

"I-I do not know what happened," Elizabeth answered, grateful for his strength. "Might I sit down, Darcy?"

Mrs. Phillips let Elizabeth's hand go. "I will fetch you something to drink," she said, before disappearing from Elizabeth's side. Carefully, Elizabeth made her way to a chair in the corner of the assembly room, sitting down with relief as she felt the weakness continue to grip her limbs.

Mr. Darcy sat down next to her, his leg pressed to hers and his eyes searching her face.

"You are unwell," he said again. "I should take you home at once."

Elizabeth grasped his hand. "Please," she said, a trifle unsteadily. "Please, do not. I will be myself again in a moment."

Mr. Darcy did not look convinced, but Elizabeth insisted again that he did not immediately call the carriage, and—much to her relief—he eventually obliged.

"I will sit with you then," he said, leaving her no room to disagree. "For the rest of the evening if I have to."

Elizabeth managed a small laugh, pressing his fingers tightly with her own. "There is no need to do so," she said, already beginning to feel a good deal better. "I am much recovered now. I feel quite well, in fact." She smiled at him, not admitting that the strange sensation that had pulled at her had, in fact, frightened her somewhat. She had never felt such a feeling before and certainly did not like the weakness that had coursed through her veins. For it to grasp her so tightly, only to flee a few moments later, left Elizabeth feeling unsteady and uncertain. Whatever could have caused such a thing?

"Here." Mrs. Phillips reappeared with a glass of water as well as a glass of champagne. "I did not know which one you would prefer, my dear."

Thanking her aunt, Elizabeth took the water and sipped it carefully, surprised that she now felt quite at ease. There was no weakness any longer, no feeling that she might faint. Instead, she felt quite herself again, as though that moment had never even occurred. The concern in Mr. Darcy's face lifted slightly, as she rose without assistance, her smile brightening her features.

"You see?" she said, as he came to stand beside her. "I am quite myself again."

This did not bring a smile to Mr. Darcy's face. "You are, perhaps, fatigued from the journey still. I ought not to have accepted an invitation so soon after arriving in London."

Elizabeth shook her head. "I would have told you if I felt too tired to attend, Darcy," she said, her voice gentle. "Do not blame yourself. It may have been that the room was a little too hot, or some trifling matter such as that. I assure you, I feel quite well again."

Mr. Darcy nodded but still did not smile. "I will remain with you for a little longer," he insisted, making Elizabeth's heart fill with warmth at his concern for her. "And should you wish to return home, you need only say the word and I shall be gone from here in a moment to fetch the carriage."

Taking his arm, Elizabeth wished they were alone so that she might press her lips to his—such was her love for him in this moment. Instead, she satisfied herself with a loving look and a whisper of love that was only for his ears, their moment together binding their hearts to each other with an even greater strength.

CHAPTER 7

"You did look a little pale last evening, Lizzie," Kitty said, sipping her steaming tea.

Elizabeth waved a hand as she sat down, grateful for the tea that was already waiting for her, the steam rising gently from the china cup.

"I was perhaps a little tired, but nothing more," she answered. "I can assure you that I am quite well today." Looking at Kitty, Mary, and Georgiana—who each had similar expressions of concern on their faces—Elizabeth gave them each a smile, although grateful for their worry for what had happened last evening.

"And you are sure you do not need to rest today?" Kitty asked, her eyes drifting to the clock on the mantlepiece. "It is not too late to cancel any particular invitations, Lizzie."

Lifting her eyebrow, Elizabeth saw Kitty flush as she caught Elizabeth's gaze. It was clear that her sister did not want to have Mr. Taylor call, but Elizabeth was not about to permit her to retract the invitation at such late notice.

"I am quite able to have Mr. Taylor—and any other person who wishes it—come to call, Kitty," she said, not budging from her stance on the issue. "I am aware that you are rather anxious over his visit, but I can assure you that there is nothing you need worry about."

Kitty swallowed hard and looked away, her jaw jutting forward just a little.

"I think Mr. Taylor spoke very well when we were first introduced to him," Georgiana chimed in, as Mary shrugged one shoulder, attempting disinterest. "I should like to know him a little better, I think."

Shaking her head, Kitty let out a sigh, looking askance at Georgiana. "But would you be so eager to have his company if you knew that he was eager to marry you?" she asked. The question was posed so bluntly and directly that Georgiana caught her breath, one hand to her mouth, as her cheeks flushed. "I am aware," Kitty continued, "that neither Lizzie nor I have spoken to you of this, Georgiana, but there is the truth of it." Biting her lip, she shook her head again, looking rather doubtful. "I am quite uncertain about him."

Elizabeth saw Georgiana's hand fall back to her lap and smiled to herself as the lady regained her composure with a steadiness that impressed Elizabeth.

"I think, Kitty," Georgiana said, after barely a moment of hesitation, "that if you are quite uncertain about him, then you should certainly allow him to call upon you and visit as many times as he wishes – until your mind becomes clear about what you seek from him."

This pleased Elizabeth greatly, for now it was not only herself who was urging Kitty to do such a thing, but Georgiana also. Mary, of course, did not appear to give much consideration to any such thing and contented herself with remaining quite silent and giving no remark on the subject whatsoever.

Heaving a great sigh of distress, Kitty put her hands to her eyes for a moment, and Elizabeth's heart twisted at her sister's upset.

"I am being foolish," Kitty said after a moment or two, her hands dropping to her lap. "He will be here within the hour, and I am aware it would be very rude to rescind the invitation at such short notice." Her eyes drifted towards Georgiana, who was wearing a sympathetic smile. "I have a great many feelings on the matter of Mr. Taylor, Georgiana, in case you have not surmised as much already!"

This lightened the mood a little, for Georgiana laughed and Kitty joined in. Elizabeth relaxed a little more into her seat, hoping eagerly that in speaking as she had done, Kitty would find a little more support from Georgiana when it came to Mr. Taylor.

"I received a letter from Mama this morning," she said, after the laughter had faded away. "She enquires after everybody's health and hopes that we are all enjoying London very much indeed." Elizabeth neglected to inform her sisters that their mother had also taken a good deal of time to complain about the fact that she herself had not been invited to London and expressed just how much she would have enjoyed being there with her daughters. It was not necessary to express those particular wishes of her mother, particularly when Elizabeth thought privately to herself that being away from Mrs. Bennet was doing both of her sisters a great deal of good.

"I confess that I do not miss Longbourn at all," Mary said suddenly, making Kitty and Elizabeth stare at her in astonishment. "I thought I would find it very difficult to be away from home for such a duration, but I find myself very content here."

Elizabeth tried to regain her composure quickly so that Mary would not think she was so surprised by her sudden revelation. “Indeed, I am glad to hear it,” Elizabeth answered quickly. “Although Mama appears to be missing you all greatly.”

“I can hardly imagine her at home, with only Father for company,” Kitty said, with a slight lilt to her voice. “Can you?”

Pausing for a moment, Elizabeth shook her head and laughed softly. “I cannot,” she said, as she smiled at Kitty. “Although, mayhap it is a good thing that she has a little experience spending time at home with only Father, for that will certainly be how things are for her one day.”

Relieved that she did not say that it would be so for Mrs. Bennet very soon, Elizabeth hid a smile, as Kitty exchanged glances with Mary, before each of them looked away. The conversation continued on for a good hour, so when the knock came at the door to announce the arrival of Mr. Taylor, none of the ladies were quite prepared to receive him.

Kitty, who, in the course of their conversation had appeared forget about Mr. Taylor’s imminent arrival, blushed furiously, and rose hastily, brushing down her skirts as she did so. Mary set down her book on a small table and did nothing more than settle her hands on her lap. Georgiana, who had been finishing the last of her tea, hurriedly set down her saucer and teacup on the tray, spilling the remnants in her hurry. Elizabeth smiled warmly at Kitty, as she set down her teacup, before calling for them to enter.

Mr. Taylor was introduced, and as he walked in, Elizabeth, Mary, and Georgiana all rose to their feet, as Kitty had already done, and curtsied to Mr. Taylor. He bowed towards them, his hands clasped in front of him but his gaze resting very firmly on Kitty.

"Good evening. I mean, good afternoon, Mrs. Darcy," he said, first speaking to Elizabeth as he ought. "And good afternoon to you also, Miss Darcy, Miss Bennet, and Miss Bennet." Greeting Kitty last, Mr. Taylor was asked to sit down and did so, just as a maid came in to take away the finished tea tray.

"Do bring another one," Elizabeth said, as the maid bobbed quickly before scurrying from the room. Turning back to Mr. Taylor, she sensed his awkwardness and smiled encouragingly, noting how he continued to glance towards Kitty, his interest in her more than apparent. This, Elizabeth considered, was not to be something she considered to be improper, but rather spoke well of his intentions towards her sister.

"How long do you intend to be in London, Mr. Taylor?" Elizabeth asked, when no one spoke a word. "Are you here for long?"

Smiling a little self-consciously, Mr. Taylor shook his head. "I cannot be far from my charge for too long," he said, spreading his hands. "My elder brother has recently married, and I was invited to London to spend a short time with them since they have now returned from their honeymoon."

"I see," Elizabeth replied, rather interested. "And he is to remain in London?"

"Yes," Mr. Taylor answered. "He is in business and has settled quite happily in London."

Silence reigned for a moment or two, and Elizabeth sent a long, stern glance towards Kitty, but her sister opened her mouth and then closed it again, appearing more than a little self-conscious.

"Might I enquire if you will be in town for some duration, Miss Bennet?" Mr. Taylor asked, turning to direct his question to Kitty. "Do you intend to return to Longbourn soon, or will you remain with your sister?"

Kitty, whose face had gone a shade of pink, looked away from Mr. Taylor but mumbled her answer. “We shall not be in town for more than a month,” she answered, her words tumbling over each other. “I do not know when I shall return to Longbourn.”

This made Mr. Taylor’s face fall, but Elizabeth doubted that her sister had noticed, given the fact that her gaze remained far from their guest.

“I see,” Mr. Taylor said, his tone now a little dulled, as he looked from Kitty to Mary and then back again. “I am sure you are enjoying your time with your sister a great deal.”

Elizabeth smiled at this remark, thinking that Mr. Taylor was a very respectable gentleman indeed. “I have been glad to have them residing with me, yes,” she answered. “It is an opportunity to speak of a good many things.” She wondered if Mr. Taylor would surmise that this meant that he himself was also discussed, a slight heat coming to her cheeks.

Thankfully, the maid soon came back into the room with a fresh tea tray, and to her relief, Mr. Darcy came after her. Rising, she greeted him warmly, before introducing him to Mr. Taylor.

“Good afternoon, Mr. Taylor,” Mr. Darcy began, bowing. “You are known to Miss Catherine Bennet, I hear.”

Mr. Taylor nodded. “I know Miss Mary Bennet also, sir,” he said, gesturing to Mary, who merely inclined her head in agreement, “but I am acquainted a little more with Miss Catherine Bennet.” He glanced at Kitty as he said this and smiled, and finally, much to Elizabeth’s relief, she finally smiled back.

"Well, I am very glad to make your acquaintance," Mr. Darcy replied, with a hint of a smile, his eyes still assessing the gentleman before him. "Are you in London for business?"

Elizabeth began to pour the tea, allowing the gentleman's conversation to fill the room as she did so. Mary took her tea with a small smile of gratitude, and Georgiana murmured her thanks. Kitty, however, said nothing at all, her lip caught between her teeth as she watched Mr. Taylor speaking with Mr. Darcy.

"Kitty," Elizabeth whispered, making Kitty start violently before she saw Elizabeth holding out a cup of tea to her.

"Thank you," Kitty whispered, before returning her gaze to Mr. Taylor and Mr. Darcy. "Lizzie, do you think that Mr. Darcy approves of him?"

Hiding a smile, Elizabeth reached down and squeezed Kitty's hand gently. "I would suggest that he does, yes," she said, seeing a flicker of relief in Kitty's eyes. "But does that matter, if *you* think him to be suitable?" She did not wait for an answer but rather resumed her seat, seeing Kitty continuing to chew on her lip.

"Then you must come to dine with us one evening," Mr. Darcy said, as Elizabeth lifted her brows in surprise, her heart filling with gladness. "I insist upon it. Bring your brother and his wife —if you wish."

Mr. Taylor looked astonished, then greatly delighted. "That is very kind of you, sir," he said, looking at Kitty, who—thankfully —did not appear to be shocked or horrified but rather kept her expression quite nonchalant. "I would be very glad to introduce them to you all."

“We shall make a dinner party of it,” Mr. Darcy said, with a broad smile that transformed his features entirely. “My dear, what do you think? Should you like to invite Mr. and Mrs. Phillips?”

Elizabeth beamed at him, glad beyond measure that her husband did not belittle those beneath his status any longer and all the more appreciative that he was suggesting such a thing—mostly for Kitty’s sake.

“I think they would be delighted to come,” she said warmly.

“Capital,” Mr. Darcy replied, with a sudden twinkle in his eye. “And have them bring Mr. Reid also...if he should like to attend.”

Elizabeth’s eyes flared wide, and she turned to Mary, seeing the color rush into her sister’s cheeks. To have a clerk sitting at a gentleman’s table was rather extraordinary indeed – but if that clerk might one day be her brother-in-law, then was it not right for them to show him kindness and welcome from the very beginning?

“Tell me about your parish, Mr. Taylor,” Georgiana said, attempting to continue the conversation when it seemed neither Kitty nor Mary had anything in particular to say. Elizabeth let out a small sigh of relief, as Mr. Taylor eagerly spoke of his charge and his parishioners. There was a clear delight in his mode of living that was coming through in his words. She thought him an excellent fellow indeed, and she prayed that Kitty’s silence came from a place of indecision and confusion rather than rejection.

All too soon it was time for Mr. Taylor to take his leave. They rose, and Mr. Taylor bowed to each of them in turn, bidding everyone farewell in a most proper manner. Elizabeth, a little frustrated that Kitty had said nothing to the gentleman at all, shot her sister a hard look, but Kitty was not even glancing in her direction. Her face was infused with color as she stepped forward, her hands twisting together as she bobbed a quick curtsy.

"Allow me to walk you to the door, Mr. Taylor," Kitty said, her voice a little higher than usual, as she kept her gaze steadfastly on a spot on the wall just past Mr. Taylor's head. "You do not mind, Lizzie?"

Elizabeth shook her head, smiling to herself. "Not in the least," she answered, as Kitty made her way towards the door, leaving a somewhat shocked Mr. Taylor to follow in her wake. He mumbled a quick farewell again, thanking Mr. Darcy again for the dinner invitation, before he left the room.

The moment the door closed, Elizabeth let out a long breath and stared, laughing softly, at Mr. Darcy.

"Well," he said, slapping both hands down upon his knees. "That was a little...unexpected."

Georgiana giggled at her brother's astonished expression. "I think that she is considering him," she said, as Mr. Darcy chuckled. "Is that not apparent?"

Elizabeth joined in their chuckles but with much more careful consideration to Kitty's actions than the others were giving. Kitty had appeared flustered but determined, and she had to confess that she was very glad to see her so. It meant that she was giving Mr. Taylor consideration, pushing aside what she once expected for herself, as well as ignoring the lingering words of their mother—and *that*, Elizabeth considered, was an excellent decision on Kitty's part.

She happened to glance across at Mary and was rather stunned to see her sitting perfectly still and rather pale faced, with wide, staring eyes, and hands clasped tightly together. It was as though she had seen what had happened with Kitty and could not quite believe it.

"Mary," she ventured, as Georgiana and Mr. Darcy continued to speak together. "Are you quite all right?"

It took a moment for her sister to gather herself, for she looked at Elizabeth with a somewhat vacant stare, which almost made Elizabeth rise from her chair and go towards her, fearing that something was seriously wrong.

"Lizzie," Mary whispered, her face now rather pinched. "Do you mean to say that Kitty is considering *accepting* that particular gentleman?"

Elizabeth looked at Mary carefully, a little taken aback by the question. "I should think so," she said gently. "You knew this, surely?"

Mary shook her head, her lip trembling for a moment as she looked away.

"You must have heard Mama speak of him," Elizabeth pressed, as Mary let out a shuddering breath. "In fact, I am certain that you have been well aware of his attachment to Kitty."

"But I did not expect her to ever truly consider him," Mary replied, with a slightly tortured look in her eyes. "The way Mama spoke, I believed that he was much too low in status to be suited to Kitty."

"That is foolishness," Elizabeth answered, but with a gentleness in her tone. "You and Kitty do not have a great fortune and neither do you have a significant dowry." Seeing Mary's frown, she tried to explain herself a little better. "What I mean to say, Mary, is that a clergyman is more than suitable for Kitty. Simply because Jane and I have married so well does not mean that the same is required for you and Kitty." Remembering what she had said to Kitty a little earlier, Elizabeth tried to express the very same to Mary. "If a gentleman is able to take care of his wife and provide for them both for the rest of their days, then that is all that is required." She lifted one shoulder in a small shrug. "I should have married Mr. Darcy if he had been a clergyman. Or, perhaps, even a clerk."

At this remark, Mary's eyes shot to Elizabeth's, and she stared at her as though Elizabeth had spoken of some great secret that was never again to be mentioned. Slowly, Elizabeth began to realize that, if Kitty was considering accepting Mr. Taylor, then Mary might begin to rethink her situation with Mr. Reid. If Kitty could consider a gentleman such as a clergyman, then there should be no reason for Mary not to consider a clerk.

Perhaps that was what had been making Mary so reluctant.

"Did you fear that you would be the lowliest of all the sisters?" Elizabeth asked, her heart suddenly aching for her sister. Mary, who had been so looked down upon by their mother, who had been berated for her lack of beauty in comparison to her sisters by Mrs. Bennet, time and again, might very easily fear that she would continue to be overshadowed by her sisters – even though there was nothing different between them all.

Elizabeth could well imagine their mother berating Mary for marrying a lowly clerk rather than find someone significantly better than that, comparing her husband to other gentlemen. One look into Mary's eyes and Elizabeth saw that she had discovered the truth.

Mary, who gave very little away in terms of how she felt, turned her head away suddenly, but not before Elizabeth had seen the tears glistening in her eyes.

"Oh, Mary," she said gently, rising from her chair and moving to sit closer to her sister. "A clerk is a perfectly respectable man. There should be no reason for you not to consider him, should you wish it."

Closing her eyes, Mary kept her head turned away. "Mother would never allow it."

"It is not Mama that you need to consider," Elizabeth told her evenly. "If Father approves of him, then that is all you need to concern yourself with."

Pressing her lips together, Mary finally glanced back at Elizabeth. "You would not look down on a gentleman such as he?"

"Certainly not," Elizabeth answered. "Can you not see that already? Mr. Darcy would not have offered to invite him to dine with us if he was not willing for his company."

Nodding slowly, Mary's color began to return to her cheeks, but her eyes became a good deal more thoughtful, looking towards Mr. Darcy as she considered this. Elizabeth was about to ask more, when the door opened and Kitty reappeared. She appeared a little ill at ease, her cheeks flushed and her eyes shifting from place to place as she strode towards her chair, only to check herself and walk to the window.

"Did you speak with Mr. Taylor?" Elizabeth asked, rising quickly and hoping that Mary would not feel as though she had been suddenly neglected. "Is all well?"

Kitty did not turn around as she continued to stand by the window, looking out at the street below.

"Indeed, all is quite well," she answered, her voice holding a tightness to it that Elizabeth had not expected. "Mr. Taylor is to dine with us, it seems, and I am to be introduced to his brother and his new wife." Her eyes did not linger on Elizabeth's face but rather returned to the street, her smile a little lackluster. "He spoke openly with me, Lizzie."

"Oh?" Elizabeth's heart quickened, but she controlled herself with an effort.

"He wanted to call on me," Kitty replied, with a heavy sigh. "Not to greet my family but rather only to visit me."

Nodding slowly, Elizabeth studied Kitty's face carefully. "And what did you say?"

Closing her eyes, Kitty shook her head. "I told him that I would be glad of his company," she said, sounding quite miserable. "His face lit up as though I had given him something quite wonderful."

Elizabeth smiled, but Kitty did not return it. "Perhaps you did," she told her sister, but Kitty merely shook her head.

"Even now, I am not convinced that it is the correct course of action," she said with a heavy sigh. "What if I do not care for him as I think I do?" Her eyes suddenly widened, and she stared at Elizabeth as though only just realizing what she had said.

Aware that she needed not to make any sort of remark about what Kitty had only just revealed, Elizabeth chose her words with great care. "If you believe that you care for him, Kitty, then the only way to be assured of it is to spend greater time in his company," she said softly. "Then you will be quite certain, I promise you."

For a moment, Elizabeth feared that Kitty was about to burst into tears, such was the glistening in her eyes, but instead, Kitty drew in a long breath and smiled rather tentatively.

"You speak from experience, I presume."

"I do," Elizabeth answered honestly, glancing over her shoulder to where Mr. Darcy was continuing to speak to Georgiana. "I will not express all that I felt and all that I feared during the time Mr. Darcy and I were acquainted, but I will truthfully tell you that I spent a good deal of time lost in confusion and doubt. I was upset, I was angry, I was heartbroken. And then, when everything became clear, I knew in my heart that to be Mr. Darcy's wife was all that I desired."

This, for whatever reason, seemed to satisfy Kitty a great deal. She sighed, but a tiny smile lingered, lifting her countenance somewhat. Elizabeth reached out and embraced her sister, feeling as though she was drawing closer to Kitty than ever before.

"It will all become clear for me also," Kitty said, hope filling her eyes as she looked into Elizabeth's face. "I must let myself believe it."

CHAPTER 8

"Good evening, Mr. Darcy."

"Good evening, Mr. Taylor."

Elizabeth smiled warmly as Mr. Taylor the clergyman introduced his elder brother, Mr. Robert Taylor, to Mr. Darcy. She saw a gentleman with very similar features to Mr. Taylor – a tall, broad-shouldered fellow with a shock of dark hair and a warm smile that reached his blue eyes. After he had been introduced to Elizabeth, he then sought to introduce his new bride, a very lovely young lady by the name of Christina.

Christina, by first appearances, seemed a little shy, but she greeted Elizabeth with grace, expressing her gratitude for her kindness in inviting her to dine with them this evening. Being of a similar height to Elizabeth, but with fair hair and vivid blue eyes, Elizabeth thought her to be very elegant indeed.

Once all the introductions had been made, there was then a short time for them to converse before dinner was served. Elizabeth watched with a growing delight in her heart as Kitty and Mr. Taylor immediately began a conversation, with Mr. Taylor expressing delight over being able to be in Kitty's company again.

"It was a little unusual for Mr. Darcy to invite my husband's clerk," said Mrs. Phillips.

Turning, Elizabeth smiled at the knowing look in Mrs. Phillips' eye.

"I am sure that you can understand why. I do hope that he feels welcome this evening," said Elizabeth.

Mrs. Phillips hesitated. "When the invitation was given, I did fear that he would not be willing to attend, given that Mr. Darcy's status is of much higher status than himself."

Understanding this, Elizabeth nodded. "But he was convinced?"

With a twist of her lips, Mrs. Phillips gestured towards her husband, who was laughing at something Mr. Robert Taylor had said. "He was, yes," she said. "My husband was most insistent, and Mr. Reid did not want to insult Mr. Darcy by refusing."

"I must hope that you understand our reasons for including him," Elizabeth replied, as Mrs. Phillips nodded. "If he is to wed my sister one day soon, then I would hope to begin our introductions well."

"That is very considerate of you," Mrs. Phillips answered, gently, "but do you truly believe that Mary might accept his attentions?"

"I am not at all sure," Elizabeth answered. "There was something that occurred recently where I believe that she may now be allowing herself to, at the very least, *imagine* the idea of accepting him. But I am not sure whether or not that will make a difference to the outcome of this situation."

Mrs. Phillips' smile faded away. "I must hope that it will," she said slowly, looking across at Mary. "I do not believe that she will be content living on her own in Longbourn – or wherever she will end up thereafter, despite what she believes."

"I am convinced of that also," Elizabeth answered. "But Mary is not easily persuaded. She must make up her own mind."

Mrs. Phillips' eyes twinkled. "A common trait in the Bennet sisters," she said, as Elizabeth blushed. "Come now, there is the bell for dinner. Let us go through. I am rather hungry already!"

~

The dinner table was set beautifully, and Elizabeth greatly enjoyed both the food and the conversation. Mr. Reid was rather quiet but managed to discuss matters that were pertinent to him whenever he felt able. Mr. Taylor appeared to be much more interested in listening to what others had to say rather than expressing his own opinions, his eyes roving around the table as each person spoke. The elder Mr. Taylor spoke a great deal, although what he had to say was always interesting and pertinent, and it seemed—based off of Mr. Darcy's expression—that he found the man to have excellent conversation. Mr. Phillips was also inclined to discuss matters at great length, which permitted Elizabeth to have a quiet conversation with Mrs. Taylor.

Kitty and Mary remained fairly silent throughout, although, upon occasion, Elizabeth noticed Mr. Taylor speaking quietly to Kitty and that Kitty, blushing furiously, answered politely. Whenever Mr. Reid spoke, however, Mary paid great attention to his words. Normally, Elizabeth would have expected Mary to speak at the most inappropriate times and usually with a rather embarrassing or impertinent remark, but this time,

Mary remained quite silent. She watched carefully and listened with great intent, looking at Mr. Reid with a rather sharp gaze.

"Your sisters are certainly quiet if you do not mind me saying so," Mrs. Taylor remarked, suddenly looking rather stricken, as though she had only just realized that she ought not to have said anything of the sort. "I do hope that they do not find the conversation dull."

Elizabeth laughed and reassured Mrs. Taylor at once. "Indeed, they are surprising me with their silence!" she said, with a smile. "I think they both have something rather weighty on their minds at present."

"Oh." Mrs. Taylor's eyes flared wide, and she darted a look at her brother-in-law. "I hope you will not think me impertinent, Mrs. Darcy, but I think my brother-in-law is very much inclined towards your sister."

"He has spoken to you of her then?" Elizabeth asked.

Mrs. Taylor nodded. "I have heard him speak of her a good many times, Mrs. Darcy," she answered, with a small smile. "There appears to be a good deal of delight in the acquaintance, and I know that he hopes for a little more from their connection."

Nodding, Elizabeth glanced at Kitty and then to Mr. Taylor, who was speaking to her again. "I am aware of that also, Mrs. Taylor," she said quietly, feeling as though she could speak honestly with the lady. "My sister has not yet decided what her feelings are on the matter, but I can assure you that I have been encouraging her to give him great consideration."

A flash of relief came into Mrs. Taylor's features. "I am very glad to hear that, Mrs. Darcy," she said honestly. "I would not ever force a lady into a decision, but I can assure you that Mr. Taylor is an excellent man and would treat her with great kindness."

"I am glad to hear of his good character," Elizabeth answered. "I have surmised as much myself, although our acquaintance has been of a very short duration."

Nothing more was said on the matter for, with the meal now finished, Elizabeth realized that Mr. Darcy was looking pointedly at her, clearly expecting now for the gentlemen to be left to their port for a time.

A little embarrassed that she had not noticed her duty before now, Elizabeth rose quickly from her chair.

"Ladies," she said, looking around the table with a welcoming smile on her face. "Might we adjourn to the drawing room? The gentlemen, I think, would be glad to be left with their port for a short time."

Mary, Kitty, Mrs. Taylor, and Mrs. Phillips rose from their seats at once, and within a few minutes, the ladies had taken their leave of the gentlemen and were sitting together in the drawing room. Trays bearing teacups and teapots now waited for Elizabeth's attention, and she quickly did her duty as the hostess.

"You look very well, Mary," Mrs. Phillips said, as Elizabeth handed her aunt a cup and saucer. "As do you, Kitty." She smiled at one and then the other. "It seems as though London suits you."

"Mayhap it is not London but the company, Aunt," Kitty said, with a shy smile that surprised Elizabeth all the more. "It has been good to see you again these last few days."

Elizabeth continued to serve the tea and finally filled one for herself, sitting down in her chair with a grateful sigh. She listened to the conversation rather than taking part in it, feeling suddenly very weary even though she had not had a good deal to do during the day.

That strange sensation of weakness suddenly overtook her again, along with a fear that she might soon cast up her accounts. Setting down her teacup hastily, so that the tea slopped over the side of the cup, she quickly whispered her excuses and hurried from the room. It seemed as though Mrs. Phillips had not noticed, given that the conversation continued behind Elizabeth's departure. She made sure to close the door quietly, one hand pressed to her stomach as she slowly made her way along the hallway, desperate to make it to the parlor.

"Lizzie!"

Mary was beside her in an instant, one hand around her shoulders.

"Your face went very pale all of a sudden," Mary said by way of explanation. "Whatever is the matter?"

Elizabeth shook her head, only to instantly regret it given the way her stomach began to churn.

"I should take you to Mr. Darcy at once," Mary said, but Elizabeth quickly refused that idea. "He is with the other gentlemen," she said, wondering why her stomach churned so. "I would not want to interrupt him. Besides," she continued, as Mary opened the door to the parlor and ushered her inside, "I am sure that it will pass in a few minutes. I must return to my guests."

Mary frowned and hurried Elizabeth into a chair, bending down to look into her face.

"What can I do?" she asked, her voice filled with urgency. "Can I call a maid?"

Elizabeth, recalling that a glass of cold water had helped the weakness to pass before, nodded. "Ask her to bring me a glass of water," she said, feeling already a little better, as she sat quietly, resting her head back against the chair. "That is all I require."

Mary rang the bell and then hurried back to Elizabeth's side, her eyes filled with worry. Elizabeth wanted to reassure her but could only close her eyes, waiting desperately for the moments of weakness to pass. Hearing the maid arrive, she did not open her eyes nor speak, concentrating all she could on pressing away the weakness.

"Here, Lizzie," Mary said.

A cold glass of water was pressed into her hands, and Elizabeth drank it quickly, suddenly feeling incredibly thirsty. Once the glass was empty, she opened her eyes and handed it back to Mary, who was still watching her with grave concern.

"How do you feel, Lizzie?" Mary asked quietly, as though raising her voice might make Elizabeth feel worse. "Are you at all recovered?"

Taking in a few long breaths, Elizabeth nodded and tried to smile. The weakness had begun to lift from her, but her stomach was still a little unsettled. "I am sure I am able to return to the others now." Rising slowly, she felt herself sway for just a moment, with Mary immediately grasping her arm.

"I am all right," she said, trying to hide the fact that she was rather afraid of what had happened for what was now the second time. "Truly, Mary, I feel much better."

Mary let go of her arm tentatively, but Elizabeth only smiled, moving towards the door of the parlor. "Come," Elizabeth continued, injecting as much confidence as she could into her voice. "The ladies will wonder where we have got to."

Following after her, Mary looped her arm through Elizabeth's and walked alongside her, still shooting her questioning glances now and again.

"I do not know what happened," Elizabeth said, hearing Mary's unasked question. "It is the second time that I have felt that strange weakness, but I do not know what it is or why it comes over me in such a manner." Shaking her head, Elizabeth allowed herself a heavy sigh. "I shall speak to Darcy about it, of course."

"This evening," Mary said, with such a firmness in her voice that Elizabeth glanced at her in surprise. "Before you retire. You must, Lizzie."

Elizabeth nodded, feeling an urge to pull Darcy aside almost at once to tell him what had happened to her, feeling that swell of fear in her chest all over again. "I will," she assured Mary, as they opened the door to the drawing room. The gentlemen, she saw, had already joined the ladies and, whilst they looked up and greeted the them as they came in, no one remarked on their absence.

However, one look towards Mr. Darcy and Elizabeth knew that he was aware that all was not well. His brow furrowed, and he made to rise, but Elizabeth quickly shook her head and walked to sit down in a chair.

"Perhaps Georgiana might entertain us on the piano?" Mr. Darcy suggested, a few minutes later. He smiled at his sister, who blushed but rose.

"I have heard that you are very accomplished," Mrs. Taylor said, glancing at Kitty and sharing a smile. "I should be very glad to hear you."

Georgiana, who had gained a little more confidence since Elizabeth had last heard her play, immediately sat down and struck up a most enjoyable tune. Everyone listened with delight, but Mr. Darcy slowly rose and made his way towards Elizabeth, coming to sit next to her as she took the seat where Georgiana had been sitting.

"You were not well?"

Elizabeth glanced at him but nodded. "I felt very weak again. It passed quickly, but I had to excuse myself for a short time."

His forehead puckered. "I think it might be wise to have a physician attend you, my dear," he said, his voice only for her ears as Georgiana continued to play. "I want you to be well—and a physician will be able to advise us about what will help you recover."

Elizabeth hesitated for a moment, wanting to tell her husband that there was nothing he needed to be concerned about, only to let out a long breath and nod her head slowly.

"Very well, Darcy," she said, as Georgiana's piece came to an end. "If you think that is for the best. Although," she finished, a trifle hesitantly, "might we wait until we return to Pemberley? I believe that your own physician would be best, rather than someone neither of us know here in London, despite how excellent their reputation may be."

Mr. Darcy paused, his expression considering, before he nodded. "Very well. But if it happens again, or if you become worse, then I must insist that we see a physician here in London."

“Thank you, Darcy,” she murmured, as Mr. Reid exclaimed that he would be very glad indeed to hear more from Georgiana. “That brings a great relief to my mind.”

“As it does to mine,” he replied, pressing her hand tightly again before Georgiana once more began to play.

CHAPTER 9

The following sennight, Elizabeth was encouraged to take a little more rest by both of her sisters, her sister-in-law, and Mr. Darcy himself, and thus, she found herself quite at her leisure. It seemed to suit her very well, for she did find herself quite fatigued and being able to rest in the afternoons did help her a great deal.

There was not a particular bout of weakness that captured her again, for which both Elizabeth and Mr. Darcy were very grateful indeed, but there was, however, a sensation of being not quite well. This, however, she hid from all her other companions in the house, and even from Mr. Darcy, not wanting him to be even more concerned for her than he already was at present.

Mr. Taylor had called upon Kitty almost every day, and Elizabeth had been present for every single visit so as to maintain propriety. However, by the end of the week, she was very rarely spoken to, such was the degree of conversation between Kitty and Mr. Taylor. This pleased Elizabeth greatly, for she was glad to see her sister so engaged and prayed that this would bring an end to Kitty's confusion and doubt.

Of Mr. Reid, however, there was very little sign. What there was, instead, were letters, which appeared for Mary both morning and evening. Mary could still be found in the library on most occasions, although Elizabeth was pleased to see Mary exerting herself a little more and going out to different places for various events. However, it had not escaped Elizabeth's notice that Mary was beginning to return Mr. Reid's letters – although certainly not at the same frequency as he!

There was an urge now to speak to her sister about her considerations of Mr. Reid, but something held Elizabeth's tongue. Perhaps it was the look in Mary's eyes as she received each letter. Or mayhap it was the quietness that had returned to her sister, who remained locked in her own thoughts for much of the day.

"Lizzie?" a voice said.

Elizabeth looked up from the book she had been reading – or trying to read, given that her thoughts were filled with that of her sisters – and saw Kitty framed in the doorway, her face a little anxious.

"Kitty?" Elizabeth enquired, making to rise. "Are you quite all right?"

Kitty came in hurriedly, gesturing for Elizabeth to remain seated. "You are not too tired, I hope?"

"Oh, not at all!" Elizabeth exclaimed, not wanting Kitty to remove herself for fear of exhausting her. "Do come in, Kitty, and do not worry about me. I am quite rested today." She smiled at her sister in reassurance, and Kitty returned it, albeit rather timidly.

"I-I wanted to tell you that Mr. Taylor is to return to Meryton," she said, her voice a little strained. "He will be returning very soon. By the end of this week."

"I see," Elizabeth murmured, seeing the sadness in Kitty's eyes and wondering if her sister knew just how obvious her sorrow over this news was. "And you do not wish him to return, I think."

Closing her eyes for a moment, Kitty took in a steadying breath. "It is foolish, is it not?"

"No, not at all," Elizabeth quickly replied. "You have only just begun to discover the truth of your true feelings for Mr. Taylor, and now, to have him gone from your side when you have been enjoying his company, it must be a little distressing."

Nodding as though to reassure herself, Kitty looked away from Elizabeth for a long moment before speaking again.

"I have come to enjoy his company, Lizzie." Her voice was quiet, as though such an admittance would make Elizabeth mock her in some way. "In fact, I shall be very sorry indeed to have him gone from my side."

Elizabeth pressed her lips together but said nothing, keeping her thoughts to herself.

"I think," Kitty continued, each word slow and careful, "that should I tell Mama that I am considering accepting Mr. Taylor's affections, that she would then do all she could to have me change my mind."

"That is true," Elizabeth answered, rather surprised that Kitty had noticed such a thing. "You know that Father, on the other hand, would be very glad indeed to give him your acceptance."

Kitty drew in a long breath and then lifted her chin. There was a hint of determination in her eyes, her resolve clear. "I think, Lizzie, that I should like to return to Pemberley with you, whenever you and Mr. Darcy seek to return," she began. "However, before Mr. Taylor departs for Meryton, I shall ask him to write to Father."

Elizabeth's heart suddenly skipped a beat, and she clasped her hands together tightly, trying desperately to keep what she had to say to herself.

"If Father gives his permission, then I shall marry Mr. Taylor," Kitty finished, her shoulders settling as she held Elizabeth's gaze. "Because, Lizzie, that is what I truly want."

"Oh, Kitty!" Elizabeth exclaimed, her hands pressed to her heart now. "Are you quite certain? Has your heart already made its choice?"

Kitty nodded, a small, slow smile beginning to spread across her face, a light lifting her countenance, and her eyes seeming to glow with happiness. "I think that I love him, Lizzie," she answered, a slight tremble in her voice as though she could barely believe what she was saying. "I find myself growing despondent that our time together has come to an end. I am eager to see him every day. I find myself thinking of him whenever we are apart, and when he told me he was to return to Meryton, my heart ached with such pain that I was forced to catch my breath!"

The feelings that Kitty described were so fervent that Elizabeth laughed aloud with delight, seeing Kitty entirely reformed now. No longer was she the silly, foolish girl that had once been. Instead, she had been considerate in her decision making, had listened to her heart, and thought upon Mr. Taylor for some time before she had made her choice.

The way she spoke of Mr. Taylor convinced Elizabeth that Kitty truly had come to care for him, and this brought her such a gladness that it filled her heart entirely. In addition, she was also pleased that Kitty recognized the foolishness of their mother in attempting to encourage Kitty to find a wealthier gentleman in place of a clergyman.

"I am truly glad for you, Kitty," Elizabeth cried, reaching out to embrace her sister, as Kitty laughed and held Elizabeth tightly. "I congratulate you on making a wise choice, and for allowing your heart to become open towards Mr. Taylor." Letting her sister go, she caught Kitty's hands and looked directly into her eyes. "I think that he cares for you a great deal, Kitty. I am sure you will be very happy with him."

A flush caught Kitty's cheeks. "He has already confessed his love for me, Lizzie," she said softly. "When I accompanied him to the door earlier this afternoon, he told me the truth of his heart, just after he gave me news of his departure."

"Then I am glad you were ready to listen to it," Elizabeth replied, squeezing Kitty's hands. "Your wisdom in this situation is quite wonderful to see."

Another quiet laugh erupted from Kitty's lips. "I did not think that I could ever be considered wise," she said with a wry smile. "But to hear you call me such a thing is...rather refreshing."

Elizabeth let go of Kitty's hands and went to sit back down. "You have shown great maturity, Kitty—truly." She smiled at her sister, who had also resumed her seat. "I do not think that you need fear what the future will hold. Whether you believe it or not, I am sure you will be an excellent clergyman's wife."

~

"And so you are to leave us, Mr. Taylor." Elizabeth saw the way Mr. Taylor looked at Kitty as this was said and was gratified to see the regret in his eyes. It was clear that his affections for Kitty were quite genuine, and Elizabeth hoped for only happiness for her sister.

"I am sorry to have to return to Meryton," Mr. Taylor began, only to look a little confused and begin to stammer. "No, no, that is not what I mean to say. Indeed, to return to my charge and my parish is something that I will be glad to return to, for that is my duty."

"I quite understand," Elizabeth tried to reassure him. "I—"

"But to be removed from your company – and particularly from Miss Catherine Bennet's company – is trying indeed," Mr. Taylor finished, appearing a little satisfied now that he had managed to explain precisely what he meant. Hiding a smile, Elizabeth acknowledged this with a nod and a quick glance towards Kitty, who was blushing prettily.

"We will be sorry to see you go, Mr. Taylor, but I am certain it will not be too long before you see Kitty again," Elizabeth said, as Mary looked from one to the other, her brows lifted and her eyes glittering with evident curiosity. Georgiana, however, appeared to know precisely what had occurred and was beaming at Mr. Taylor, clearly quite delighted for them both whilst Mr. Darcy remained standing near to the fireplace, nodding his head in agreement with what Elizabeth had just expressed.

Elizabeth knew that her husband was pleased for Kitty but also that his expressions did not always convey the happiness that he felt. Mr. Taylor had glanced at him already on a few occasions, but Mr. Darcy had neither smiled nor inclined his head towards him as yet.

"And you will have to visit us at Pemberley," Mr. Darcy said suddenly, his voice and presence filling the room, as Mr. Taylor's eyes widened in astonishment, staring at Mr. Darcy as though he could hardly believe what he had heard. "Once all is settled, of course," Mr. Darcy finished, with a small shrug of one shoulder.

This appeared to be a very great relief to Mr. Taylor, who bowed his head and expressed his thanks on more than one occasion, making Mr. Darcy frown in confusion and Elizabeth laugh softly to herself at the expression on her husband's face. It was not his fault that he was a rather staid sort, but she knew very well that he could be intimidating simply by standing in a room. She would have to explain to him why Mr. Taylor had appeared relieved a little later.

"I should take my leave," Mr. Taylor said, suddenly rising to his feet and looking directly at Kitty. "I do not want to miss the stage."

"But of course." Elizabeth rose from her chair and bid Mr. Taylor farewell, just as Mary and then Georgiana had done. Mr. Darcy again expressed his wish that Mr. Taylor visit them at Pemberley when the right time came, and Mr. Taylor again thanked him with such exclamations that it seemed to almost overwhelm Mr. Darcy.

"I shall accompany you to the door," Kitty said, glancing at Elizabeth for her approval, which she gave almost at once. With a smile pulling at her lips, she watched Kitty and Mr. Taylor depart the room – although the door was left wide open, just as she expected.

"How glad I am for them," Georgiana sighed, as she settled herself back into her chair. "I think that Kitty has made a very wise choice."

"As do I," Elizabeth agreed. "Mr. Taylor clearly cares for her, and I am sure he will be able to provide a suitable home and income for them both."

Mr. Darcy chuckled, his expression changing almost immediately. "I confess that, the first time I met your sister, I never once considered that she would marry a clergyman," he said and laughed, as the others – save for Mary – joined in. "To have her as the wife of a clergyman is almost a little difficult to believe!"

"But I believe she will do very well," Elizabeth replied, a trifle defensively. "She has shown great maturity now, and I think that she will continue to develop her character in much the same way during her marriage."

Mr. Darcy's smile was tender. "I am certain that you are right, my dear," he said with a half bow. "I know that you are very happy for her, and I am pleased to admit that I feel very much the same happiness also." He glanced towards the door. "I should follow after them, I think."

"They have had a few minutes," Elizabeth agreed, watching her husband as he left the room, glad that he felt as much joy as she.

Silence reigned for a few minutes. Georgiana looked very content indeed, whereas Mary stared straight ahead, her hands clasped tightly together in her lap. Elizabeth, catching her sister's evidently shocked expression, watched her with interest for a few minutes. Had Mary not realized that Kitty had been considering Mr. Taylor with great deliberation? Or perhaps she *had* realized such a thing but then believed that her sister would refuse him.

"Mary?" She looked at her sister steadily, as Mary's eyes flicked towards her, her hands still clutched tightly together. "Mary, are you quite all right?"

"Quite." Mary's voice was sharp, her expression tight. "I am quite all right."

"It is only," Elizabeth continued, as gently as she could, "that you appear rather shocked about such news."

Mary said nothing for a moment or two, looking at Elizabeth with a hard gaze. It was, Elizabeth felt, as though she had done some great wrong, and Mary now expected her to try and realize such a thing of her own accord.

"I am a little surprised, that is all," Mary said eventually, rising from her chair in a flurry of skirts. "If you will excuse me. I think I shall return to the library."

Unable to say anything more, unable to find the words to convince Mary to stay and to speak of whatever was lingering on her mind, Elizabeth watched her departure with a heavy heart. Wishing she could have found the right words to say, Elizabeth sighed and lowered her eyes to her lap, wondering how she could find out what was troubling Mary so.

"I think she is uncertain over Mr. Reid," Georgiana said, evidently seeing Elizabeth's confusion. "The letters have been coming every day, as you know, and she has been answering them."

"I am aware that she has been replying to him," Elizabeth replied, looking at Georgiana and seeing the gentleness in her eyes. "But I had hoped that it meant she was almost ready to accept him."

Georgiana shook her head. "I think she is still greatly troubled about what she should do. I have not spoken to her a great deal, but the letters are an indication that she is certainly considering him but is uncertain as to whether or not a clerk is the correct sort of husband."

Elizabeth closed her eyes, the frustration rising suddenly. "A clerk is not unsuitable."

"And I believe," Georgiana continued softly, "that having had no feelings of this kind before, she now finds herself to be very uncertain indeed about whether or not they are of the lasting kind."

Nodding slowly, Elizabeth took in a long breath and let it out again, pushing her frustrations away. "Seeing Kitty so content and certain, however, must make her eager to then find her own satisfaction."

"And exasperated when she cannot," Georgiana quietly agreed. "There is a good deal for Mary to battle with. I do not think she likes being in this state of confusion, in this strange uncertainty. Thus, to see Kitty in such a state of joy, her decisions made without evident hesitation, it must make her a good deal more frustrated."

"I should say something to her," Elizabeth murmured, half to herself. "I just do not know what I should say."

Georgiana watched her for a few moments, evidently aware of Elizabeth's difficulties in considering what she ought to say to assist Mary in her trial. "I... If I do not speak out of turn, Lizzie, I would suggest that you wait until Mary comes to speak to you about matters of the heart," she said gently. "I do not know Mary particularly well, but whenever she has mentioned something of Mr. Reid to me, it has been of her own volition."

It went against Elizabeth's own considerations to leave Mary alone and not to go in search of her to speak openly, but she forced herself to consider what Georgiana had said, rather than merely following her own advice.

"It is difficult, I know," Georgiana continued, as though she could tell what Elizabeth was thinking. "But I do believe it will be for the best."

Rubbing at her forehead for a moment, Elizabeth nodded slowly and saw how Georgiana smiled. "I must hope that she will say something soon," she replied, as Georgiana nodded. "For we are to return to Pemberley in a fortnight, and if matters are not settled between herself and Mr. Reid by then, I do not know what will happen next!"

"Then I shall pray that everything will come to rights," Georgiana replied, speaking practically as always. "And that, when the time comes, you will know precisely what to say."

Elizabeth thought this a very kind expression from her sister-in-law and told her so. Georgiana made to reply, only for Mr. Darcy to come back into the room, followed by Kitty, who was practically glowing with happiness.

"It is all settled," Kitty told them, without waiting for anyone to ask. "Mr. Taylor is to write to Father this very day!" She clasped her hands together tightly at her heart, her eyes aglow with joy. "I am sure that within the week I shall hear from Father that all is just as I now hope."

"And so another wedding shall soon take place," Elizabeth finished, getting out of her seat to embrace her sister, with Georgiana following suit. "How marvelous, Kitty!"

Kitty laughed and pressed Elizabeth's hands. "It is all more wonderful than I could have hoped," she said softly. "Thank you, Lizzie, for all that you have said and done to aid me through this. I do not think I could have reached this place in my life without you."

"I am very glad for you, indeed," Elizabeth replied. "And may you experience this joy every single day of your life with Mr. William Taylor."

~

"You have not had any more turns?"

Elizabeth looked up in surprise as Mr. Darcy came into her adjoining bedchamber, an anxious look on his face.

"Darcy," she said gently, reaching out one hand to him. "I would have told you if I had experienced such a thing."

His eyes searched her face. "I fear that you seek to protect me, Elizabeth," he said softly, his fingers holding tightly to hers. "You would rather not tell me the truth for fear of what I will think."

"I have not had any more bouts of weakness," she told him firmly, although a small niggle of guilt came into her mind, reminding her that she had not told him about the strange feeling of being rather unwell that seemed to linger within her for many hours.

Mr. Darcy nodded, holding her gaze steadily. "And you are still in agreement that the physician should come to examine you once we return to Pemberley?"

She nodded, and the worry began to fade from his eyes. "Yes, of course," she promised quietly. "I should be glad to receive him the very day we return, if you so wish."

This appeared to convince Mr. Darcy all the more, for he let out a heavy breath and ran one hand over his forehead, his eyes holding hers steadily. "I am deeply concerned for you, Elizabeth," he said tenderly, his free hand settling over their joined ones. "I cannot bear to see you unwell."

Reaching out, Elizabeth brushed her hand down his cheek, seeing how he closed his eyes at her touch, leaning into her hand as though he needed her to be there, needed to have her close to him.

"I will be well again very soon, I am sure," Elizabeth said softly, looking deeply into his eyes. "There is nothing you need to worry about, I am sure of it." With a small smile, she pressed his fingers. "I am sure it was just fatigue from the journey to London and all that came with it," she said, even though she knew in her heart that such a thing was not quite true. "Perhaps, back in Pemberley, back home, I shall be myself again completely."

"I must hope so," came Mr. Darcy's reply. "Mayhap we should return there sooner than we have planned."

Elizabeth shook her head, knowing that it would not benefit Mary to return to Pemberley without having some resolve to the matter with Mr. Reid. "I can wait a little longer," she said firmly. "I enjoy being in London, truly. And we are to go to Mrs. Maystone's dinner in a few days, remember?"

Mr. Darcy arched one eyebrow. "I would far prefer to keep you safe and content in Pemberley rather than go to another dinner," he said tenderly, lowering his head to kiss her. "You need only say the words, and I shall make the arrangements immediately."

"I know you would do so," she said, thinking that he was truly the most wonderful husband. "Thank you, Darcy."

CHAPTER 10

"Mary?"

Their last few days in London had gone rather well, Elizabeth considered, as she looked around the townhouse in search of Mary. Kitty, whilst desperately waiting for a letter from either her father or Mr. Taylor, was easily distracted from her thoughts by a variety of exciting occasions, so she did not have much opportunity to be melancholy.

Elizabeth, whilst certainly still feeling ill upon occasion, had not had any further bouts of weakness, although Mr. Darcy still insisted that she rest whenever she could. Elizabeth had not wanted to do so but had found herself grateful for the opportunity, finding that the fatigue that had grasped at her so strongly still lingered.

Georgiana had begun to speak of Pemberley again, clearly beginning to long to return home, and Mr. Darcy himself seemed very glad indeed at the thought – although whether that was because Elizabeth would finally see a physician or because of the sheer joy of returning there, Elizabeth could not say.

"Yes, Lizzie?" Mary responded.

Elizabeth walked into the small parlor, where she found Mary sitting by the window, a letter in her lap and a rather melancholy look on her face. There was no smile of greeting on her lips, no flicker of interest in her eyes. Rather, there was just a somewhat neutral expression, although Elizabeth quickly caught how Mary placed one hand atop the letter, as if she wanted to hide it from Elizabeth's notice.

"Mary," Elizabeth said, sitting down opposite her sister. "I wanted to inform you that we are to go back to Pemberley in two days' time."

Mary, who had been expecting this, merely nodded. "Yes, I knew of our departure already."

"And you will be glad to return to Pemberley?" Elizabeth asked, feeling a little anxious as she looked at her sister carefully. "Or should you wish to go back to Longbourn? I can assure you that neither Darcy nor I would be upset or troubled if you chose to return home, so do not let that hinder you."

For a few minutes, Mary said nothing. She looked back at Elizabeth with a sharp eye, as though trying to assess whether or not she ought to speak truthfully. Her hand tightened on the letter, the paper crinkling just a little, and Elizabeth could not help but glance at it.

"Mr. Reid has asked to write to Father," Mary said eventually. "I do not know what to tell him."

"I see," Elizabeth replied, wanting to support her sister in this moment but certainly not at all eager to make the decision for her. "What are your thoughts, Mary?" She was about to state that there was no need for Mary to tell her of them if she did not wish to, but before she could do so, Mary immediately began to speak.

"My heart is very much inclined towards Mr. Reid," she began, lifting her hand and revealing the letter in all its entirety. "His words are genuine, I believe, and I am very eager to continue on the acquaintance."

Elizabeth nodded and said, "I can well understand that."

"But Mama does not want him to be my husband," Mary said slowly. "And I am not certain that a clerk will be suitable for me."

Waiting for a moment, Elizabeth spoke with great care. "What is it about him being a clerk that you believe is unsuitable?"

"He.... I...." Frustrated, Mary dropped her head, running one hand over her face. "It is very odd, is it not? That Kitty should be the one to marry a clergyman."

A little alarmed, Elizabeth pressed one hand to her chest. "You do not have feelings for Mr. Taylor, surely?"

Thankfully, Mary's lips quirked, her eyes sparkling for a moment. "No, I am glad to say I do not," she answered, as Elizabeth let out a breath of relief. "But I always thought...well, I presumed that if I ever were to marry, it would be to someone with such a profession as that."

"And a clerk is not what you expected," Elizabeth finished, as Mary nodded, looking a little embarrassed. "It is taking you a little time to resolve such feelings within yourself, yes?"

"That is it precisely," Mary answered, closing her eyes as though she was a little embarrassed. "I keep telling myself that I am being foolish, that Mr. Reid is very kind indeed and clearly determined to give me the best life he can, but there is still a niggling doubt in my mind."

Elizabeth leaned forward in her chair and fixed Mary with a firm gaze. "Mary, you will not be looked down upon just because you have married a clerk," she said, remembering how Mary had spoken of feeling as though she were the least of her sisters in the eyes of her mother. "No one will look down upon you. No one will think the less of you. Rather—and I can assure you of this—everyone will be very glad for you indeed."

Mary bit her lip. "Lydia will not."

"Lydia has chosen her own path," Elizabeth replied steadily. "Her choices could have damaged all of us. Even if she does think poorly of you, do not allow her opinion to affect you. Each of us must make our own choices and build our own lives in any way we choose. This is *your* choice, Mary. Do not consider what Lydia will say or even what Mama will say. Rather, think about what *you* wish for."

"I wish to be married," Mary sighed, passing a hand over her eyes. "Mr. Reid has offered me that. He has offered me his heart. But what if my own..." Trailing off, she looked across at Elizabeth with desperation in her eyes. "What if my own heart never feels the same depth of feeling as his? He clearly has a deep affection for me, and yet, whilst I certainly feel *something* for him, it is not as great as what he has expressed for me."

"But that may come in time," Elizabeth replied gently. "And might I remind you that not every marriage is borne out of a great and glorious affection? Even our own parents, for example, were not deeply in love when they wed. But yet, there is an affection between them that can still be seen, even though our mama drives our father simply mad at times!"

This made Mary smile, and she nodded but looked away. “I fear that Mama will try to convince Father not to allow the connection,” she said softly. “What if she—?”

“Father will not permit her to, as well you know,” Elizabeth replied firmly. “His strength of character is much greater than hers. If he considers a clerk to be quite suitable for you, then he shall agree without hesitation.”

Mary nodded slowly, biting her lip again. Elizabeth remained in silence, choosing not to say anything further but rather holding her own counsel whilst Mary considered things.

“I think it would be only fair to inform Mr. Reid of my decision before I return to Pemberley,” she said after a few minutes. “Which means I must make my decision very soon.”

Elizabeth nodded. “I think you will feel a little relieved by the time you do so,” she told her sister, as Mary gave her a half smile. “Just as Kitty has done.”

Mary laughed softly. “She is certainly very pleased with her choice,” she said, as Elizabeth nodded her agreement. “I am glad for her. I did not think she would *ever* be content with a clergyman. I thought she would seek out someone akin to Wickham.”

“I think Kitty has a little more sense in her now,” Elizabeth replied, with a knowing smile. “But yes, I think her choice to be an excellent one. I look forward to what the future holds for them both.”

~

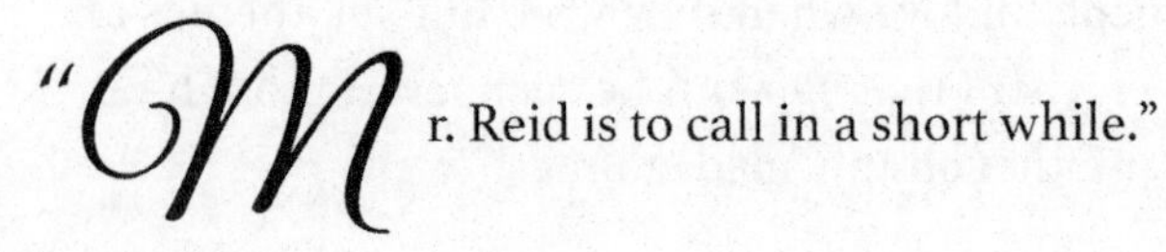

“Mr. Reid is to call in a short while.”

Elizabeth lifted her head from where she had bene putting a final few things into a bag. "Oh."

"I should have asked him to call a little earlier, I know," Mary replied, looking a little self-conscious. "But I *have* thought of this for some time, Lizzie, and I had to be quite certain."

"That is quite all right, Mary," Elizabeth replied, relieved that her sister had, in fact, made something of a decision rather to continue letting the letters come towards her, unhindered. "Might I ask what you want to do?"

Mary paused, then smiled. "I have considered everything you have said, Lizzie, and I believe it was all very wise indeed. However, I cannot pretend that my affections are the very same as his, for they do not have the strength nor the fortitude that he claims to have for me."

"I do not think this will push him far from you, Mary," Elizabeth answered honestly. "I would be glad to be with you, when it comes time to convey such a thing to him however."

This appeared to be precisely what Mary had hoped for. "I thank you, Lizzie," she said in an almost humble manner. "He will be here an hour before we depart."

"Then I shall be ready."

~

Elizabeth had not expected to feel so nervous, but when Mr. Reid walked into the drawing room to speak to Mary, she found herself rather anxious. Her hands twisted together as she sat down, turning her head away just a little as she picked a book that had been provided precisely for this occasion.

"Good afternoon, Mr. Reid," Mary said softly.

"Good afternoon," came the reply. "I am sorry to see you preparing to go, but I have been glad of your company for these last few weeks."

Silence reigned for a moment or two, and Elizabeth fought the urge to send a sidelong glance towards them both.

"I think, Mr. Reid, that I should like you to write to me again, if you would." Mary's words had become a little quicker, her voice a little higher. "I should, however, inform you that whilst I have been enjoying our correspondence, I do not believe that my affections have anywhere near the depth of your own."

Again, there came that tense, awkward silence that filled the room. Elizabeth closed her eyes tightly, praying desperately that Mr. Reid would understand what Mary was trying to say.

"I see," came the rather gruff reply. "Then, I presume, you would not wish for me to write to your father."

"Oh, the contrary," Mary replied. Her words came so quickly that Mr. Reid barely had time to finish his sentence. "I should be very glad indeed if you would do so."

Elizabeth kept her eyes closed, the book lying quite forgotten in her hand.

"You *wish* for me to write to your father, Miss Bennet?"

"Yes," Mary replied abruptly. "Yes, Mr. Reid, I should like it very much. What I mean to express is that, whilst I do not believe that my affections have anywhere near the fervor that you seem to hold within your heart, I pray that my own heart will, one day soon, follow suit. It is just not as you are at present, and that, I fear, may be something of a barrier to our suggested progress."

Wincing, Elizabeth pressed her lips together tightly. It was not quite as clear as Mary had explained to Elizabeth, and the quietness that came from Mr. Reid told her that he probably did not fully understand what Mary had been saying.

She wanted to throw herself to her feet, to cry out that Mary was doing all she could to express to Mr. Reid that she *did* care for him, but with less of a passion than he, but she forced herself to remain quiet and unobserved. This was not something that she needed to do but rather something that she had to allow Mary to do alone.

"So, you do *not* wish for me to write to your father?" Mr. Reid sounded terribly confused. "Or do you wish me to write to him a little later, when you have had a little more time?"

Elizabeth heard a long, exasperated breath come from Mary and wished desperately that she could help her.

"No, that is not what I mean at all," Mary exclaimed, sounding quite frustrated. "What I am trying to express, Mr. Reid, is that I would accept your proposal, so long as you understand that, whilst my affections *are* engaged, they are not as passionate as your own!"

Allowing herself a small smile, Elizabeth forced her gaze to the book in her hand and tried not to listen any further.

"I quite understand, Miss Bennet." Mr. Reid's voice was almost breathless. "I am grateful for your explanation but, rather than feeling as though I am at some sort of disadvantage, I instead feel greatly blessed. Blessed that you have agreed, of course, but also that your affections are engaged."

"But they are not as strong as your own," Mary protested, as though she could not believe that Mr. Reid did not appear to be upset by this in any way. "Are you sure that you—?"

"I will write to your father this very day!" Mr. Reid exclaimed, and out of the corner of her eye, Elizabeth saw him grasp Mary's hands. "This is more than I could have ever hoped for, Mary. Truly, you have made me the happiest man in all of England!"

Elizabeth smiled with relief, her chest no longer tight with tension. Mary had spoken well, and now, it seemed, all was at an end. She turned back towards Mary as Mr. Reid took his leave, bidding him good afternoon before coming to sit beside Mary.

"It seems he was not as concerned as you," Elizabeth murmured, as Mary sat there, her mouth a little open and her face white with evident surprise. "Your worries and fears were for nothing."

Mary blinked rapidly. "And now," she whispered, half to herself, "it seems that I am engaged."

Elizabeth nodded, reaching across to take Mary's hand. "You are," she answered softly, praying that Mary was not about to turn around and cry out that she regretted speaking to Mr. Reid in such an open fashion. "And I am very glad for you."

Her shoulders slumping, Mary let out a long breath, then bent forward, her expression crumpling. Her hand was pulled from Elizabeth's as she began to cry, her hands covering her face. Nonplussed, Elizabeth watched for a moment, only to put her arm around Mary's back and begin to murmur words of encouragement.

"It is a good thing, Mary, is it not?" she said, trying to be as encouraging as possible. "You hoped that he would not turn away from you over this, I am sure, and now—"

"Oh, Lizzie!" Mary exclaimed, looking up and then throwing her arms about Elizabeth's shoulders. "Lizzie, I am so very happy."

For a moment, Elizabeth froze, and then a broad smile spread across her face as she held Mary close.

"I am so very glad to hear you say that, Mary," she said, realizing that she had never seen nor experienced an outburst such as this from Mary before. "Truly, my heart is filled with joy for you. I am sure that you will be very happy with Mr. Reid."

Mary sobbed for a few minutes longer before she finally let Elizabeth go, but the smile on her face was a beautiful one. Truly, Elizabeth thought to herself, she had never seen her sister so happy.

"Mama will be furious," Mary exclaimed, a rueful smile on her face. "For Kitty to marry a clergyman and for me to wed a clerk – she will think us quite done for."

Elizabeth did not refute this, knowing quite well that this was, in fact, quite true. "Well, I shall not think such a thing—and neither will Jane or Kitty. We shall be very glad to see you so happy, Mary."

With a long but content sigh, Mary squeezed Elizabeth's hands and then rose. "I think I shall go to tell Kitty and Georgiana at once," she said, clasping her hands together and sounding like some sort of excited child. "You do not mind, Lizzie?"

"No, not in the least," Elizabeth assured her, finding her heart full with joy as she watched Mary leave. Truly, this had been the most wonderful day!

CHAPTER 11

"Are you glad to be home?"

Elizabeth sighed happily as Pemberley came into view. She looked first at Kitty, then at Mary, and finally at Georgiana, who had asked the question.

"Indeed," she said, reaching across to press Georgiana's hand. "I am *very* glad to be returned to Pemberley."

Kitty tilted her head. "And do you now consider it your home, Lizzie?"

The answer came to Elizabeth immediately. "I do," she said softly. "Mr. Darcy has done his utmost to make me feel as though I belong here, and I can easily admit that it did not take long for this place to enter my heart."

Mary smiled, her countenance still bright from the wonderful news she had shared with Mr. Reid. "I must begin to think of *London* as my home now," she said, looking out of the window. "I can hardly believe that I shall be returned there in a short time in order to wed Mr. Reid."

Georgiana giggled, one hand to her mouth. "Your father has not yet responded to Mr. Reid's letter, Mary," she said, her eyes twinkling. "Are you so certain of his agreement?"

Mary laughed too. "I am *more* than certain of it," she said, as Elizabeth nodded in agreement. "In fact, I am certain that my father will reply to Mr. Reid on the very same day he receives the letter!"

"And I am hoping that there is a letter waiting for me," Kitty said, sounding a little wistful. "Father will have received Mr. Taylor's letter by now."

"I am sure he will have written to you with as much urgency as you expect," Elizabeth answered, seeing Kitty's smile being rather tense as she looked from the carriage window to Elizabeth and back again. "The answer you receive will be as you expect, I am quite certain of it."

Kitty nodded but did not say another word until the carriage had rolled up to the doors of Pemberley. Elizabeth let out a long sigh as the carriage door opened and Mr. Darcy held out his hand to her, having ridden back to Pemberley on his horse.

"My dear," he said, as she took his hand. "We are returned home."

Her smile firmly fixed to her face, Elizabeth stepped out of the carriage and looked up at Pemberley, before turning around to take in the grounds and the familiar sights that had begun to mean so much to her. Her heart was quite full, she realized, turning back to look into Darcy's face and seeing the sheer happiness in his eyes as he smiled back at her.

"You were not unwell in the carriage, I hope?" he asked, as they climbed the steps together. "You do look a little pale."

Elizabeth hesitated before she answered, looking up at her husband for a moment. "I have felt a little unwell for some time," she confessed. "I am able to eat, however, and it is just a general feeling of being unsettled. It has lingered, however, and I have not felt myself ever since that second bout of weakness."

Mr. Darcy's eyes flared, and he began to speak, protesting that Elizabeth had not told him such a thing before.

"I know that you would have preferred to know such a thing before now," Elizabeth interrupted, "but as I have said, I was able to continue on without any particular difficulty. Besides which, if it had become worse, I would have told you at once."

Mr. Darcy's lips twitched, as he looked down at her. "You are the most frustrating and yet the most incredible lady I believe I have ever known," he said, bending down to kiss her quickly before the other ladies came in after them. "But the doctor shall be called this very afternoon."

Knowing that she could not argue with him and knowing that speaking to a physician might, in fact, relieve a little of her own worries, Elizabeth nodded and agreed without hesitation.

"A letter, Miss Bennet," said the butler.

Elizabeth turned to see Kitty accepting a letter from the butler, who then came to Mr. Darcy to inform him that tea and refreshments had been laid out in the drawing room for them all. Her stomach tightening for a moment, Elizabeth watched Kitty break open the letter, believing that she already knew precisely what was in the letter. Kitty's hand flew to her mouth, tears pooling in her eyes as she lifted her head and looked directly at Elizabeth.

"He has given Mr. Taylor his permission!" she cried, as Mary and Georgiana exclaimed with delight and embraced Kitty at once as tears of joy spilled from her eyes. "I am to be married!"

Overwhelmed with happiness for her sister, Elizabeth moved forward quickly to embrace Kitty, more joyful than she could express. "How wonderful!" she cried, as the ladies continued to exclaim in delight. "I am very happy for you, Kitty."

"This is the most joyous day," Mr. Darcy added, a smile on his face as he came to join them. "And I wish you the very same happiness that I have found in matrimony." His hand slipped around Elizabeth's waist, and she smiled up at him, leaning into his side and feeling the very same happiness within her heart as he had only just described.

~

"You have been feeling unwell, I understand, Mrs. Darcy."

Elizabeth nodded, grateful when the physician gestured for her to sit down. Apparently, there was not to be a physical examination as yet.

"Might you be able to tell me precisely what is wrong?" the physician asked, his blue eyes twinkling behind his spectacles. "What have you been feeling?"

Starting from the very first bout of weakness, Elizabeth explained how she had felt. "That only happened on two occasions," she said, as the doctor nodded sagely. "Thereafter, my husband insisted that I take a little more rest."

"And the bouts of weakness did not return once you did so?"

"I have had none since," Elizabeth confirmed. "Although I confess that I have had a lingering feeling of...being unwell."

One of the doctor's white bushy eyebrows rose. "In what way?"

This was harder to explain than Elizabeth had first expected. "I am able to eat just as normal," she began slowly, "but there is a feeling deep within my stomach that simply will not settle. As though I am on the rolling sea without any comfort."

"And this lingers all through the day?"

She nodded, a clutching fear suddenly in her stomach as she saw him frown. Whatever was wrong with her? "Do...do you need to examine me now?" she asked, only for the doctor to chuckle and shake his head. This astonished her greatly, and she stared at him, wondering what could be so funny at a time like this.

"My dear Mrs. Darcy, this malady will resolve itself in, most likely, a matter of months," he said, rising to his feet and coming towards her. "Might I enquire as to when your last courses were?"

Heat flooded Elizabeth's face at the question, but try as she might, she could not quite recall when such a thing had taken place. Her mouth fell open as she stared at the doctor, feeling such a flare of embarrassment that she did not know what to say.

"You need not feel foolish," the doctor said, patting her shoulder gently. "It is something that can, very often, slip a lady's mind when they are caught up with so many other things. Now," he finished, as Elizabeth rose, a trifle unsteady as she took in what all of this meant. "Do you wish to inform your husband or shall I?"

Elizabeth shook her head, hardly able to breathe. "I-I should like to tell him, I think."

"Excellent," the physician smiled, as he made his way to the door. "I shall return in a few weeks to examine you further, but until then, continue to rest just as you have been doing."

"I shall, of course," Elizabeth replied, tears beginning to fill her eyes as she thought of this new life formed within her, the wonderful news that she now had to share with her husband beginning to fill her.

"Elizabeth!" Mr. Darcy was at the door in a moment, his eyes wide as he stared at her. "Whatever is wrong? The physician said that you would inform me of his deliberations." He hurried forward, worry written into every line on his face as he grasped her hands. "Goodness, you are crying!" With a trembling hand, he brushed her tears away, searching her face. "Please, tell me what is wrong."

"Oh, Darcy," Elizabeth whispered, reaching up with one hand to press it lightly against his face. "Nothing is wrong. I can assure you, nothing is wrong at all. In fact, it is all quite wonderful."

Mr. Darcy stared at her, clearly not understanding what she meant.

"The doctor said this malady will pass in a few short months," she whispered, taking his hand and pressing it lightly to her stomach. "Do you understand now, my love?"

Taking in a shuddering breath, Mr. Darcy looked down at where his hand was pressed and then, slowly, began to lift his eyes to hers again, hope and joy blazing in them.

"It is true," Elizabeth whispered, tears beginning to fall down her cheeks again. "We are to welcome a child into our family,

Darcy."

Mr. Darcy closed his eyes tightly. "A baby," he breathed, his voice breaking with emotion. "Can it truly be so?"

She laughed and threw her arms about his neck, as his arms went about her waist. "It is," she whispered, her lips close to his ear. "We are to be parents."

"I can hardly believe it," he replied, pulling back gently so that he could look into her face. "I am, of course, greatly relieved to know that you are not unwell as I feared."

Laughing, Elizabeth shook her head, her heart beating with nothing other than sheer joy. "There is nothing that we need fear now," she told him, reaching up to frame his face with her hands. "You shall become a father very soon, Mr. Darcy, and an excellent father you shall be."

This appeared to be a little too much for Mr. Darcy to take, for he did not answer immediately but rather swallowed hard, clearly trying to take in this particular news.

"And we shall be very happy indeed," Elizabeth assured him, as the color began to return to Mr. Darcy's face. "Of that, I have absolutely no doubt."

"Indeed we shall," he said, his hands now about her waist as he held her close. "It will take me a little time to become used to considering myself as a father, to think of the responsibilities that will then be mine, but knowing that I have you beside me will bring me all the relief I need."

"I love you, Darcy," Elizabeth told him, seeing the tenderness and love in his eyes. "With all of my heart."

"As I love you," he replied, before leaning down to kiss her.

THE END

FREE EBOOK

Receive a FREE inspirational Regency Ebook by visiting our website and signing up for our emailing list.
Click the link to enter www.HisEverLastingLove.com in your web browser.

The newsletter will also provide information on upcoming new books and new music.

THANK YOU!

Thank you so much for reading our book. We hope you enjoyed it.

If you liked this book, we would really appreciate a five star review on Amazon or Goodreads. Every review you take the time to write makes an enormous impact on our writers' lives. Reviews really encourage our authors and let them know the positive things you enjoyed about their creativity.

Thank you again! I hope this book brightened your day.

ADDITIONAL BOOKS

Books by His Everlasting Love Media:

Historical Clean Romance:

Jane Austen's Pride and Prejudice Clean and wholesome Continuation:

- Love and Illness find Pemberly
- Love and a Scoundrel at Pemberly

Sets:

- Regency Brides Box Set
- Love for Lords Box Set
- Regency Engagements Box Set
- Lady Angelica Landerbelt Romance Collection

Charlotte Fitzwilliam:

- Wanted by the Duke
- The Marquess who Chose Me

- The Earl's Heart
- The Duke's Daughter
- Lords, Love and Stolen Jewels
- Lords, Love and Secrets
- Lords, Love and Lies
- Lords, Love, and Rivalry

Eliza Heaton:

- Care of the Duke
- The Duke's Baby
- My Secret Duke
- Infatuated with the Duke's Daughter
- Dance with a Duke's Son
- Rescued by the Duke of Brighton

Contemporary Clean Romance:

- Anne Marie Sampson
- Crush on the Shy Guy

ABOUT THE AUTHOR

Eliza Heaton grew up enjoying the amazing landscapes of her hometown in Perth, near Edinburgh, Scotland. She often visited the Isle of Skye with her parents during her summers as a child and dreamed of becoming a writer. She attended university in Edinburgh where she completed her Masters in English Literature with a focus on the Victorian and Regency periods.

Eliza currently lives in the Dean Village area of Edinburgh, Scotland, where she can walk along the Water of Leith creating the characters for her books. Cathedrals, statues of viscounts, and castles welcome her as she walks and imagines the perfect love story to write next.

Printed in Great Britain
by Amazon